Mudbug Tales
A Novel In Flashes, Wit' Recipes

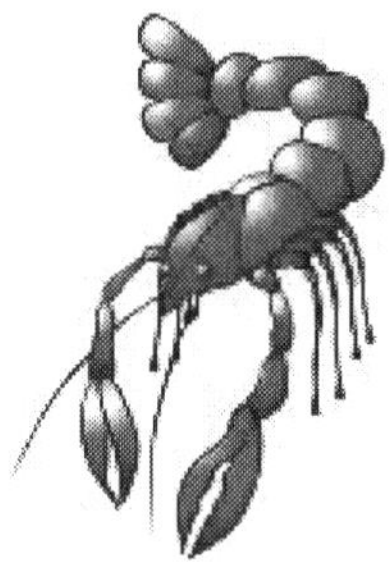

GC Smith

Century Oak Publishing

Century Oak Publishing

Mudbug Tales
A Novel In Flashes,
Wit' Recipes

Published at Createspace by GC Smith,
Century Oak Publishing

Primary Category: Fiction /Literary, Folklife, Food, Cookbook
Country of Publication/ United States
Language/ English

ISBN-13:
978-1499716849

ISBN-10:
1499716842

Search/ Keywords: Cajun, Folklife, Louisiana, Food, Cookbook, Crawfish, Mudbug

Century Oak Publishing

Century Oak Publishing

For Ramon "Ray" Collins
my friend and formerly the publisher
of the e-zine Quiction
through which many
MUDBUG TALES
first saw the light of day

MUDBUG TALES
A NOVEL IN FLASHES
WIT' RECIPES

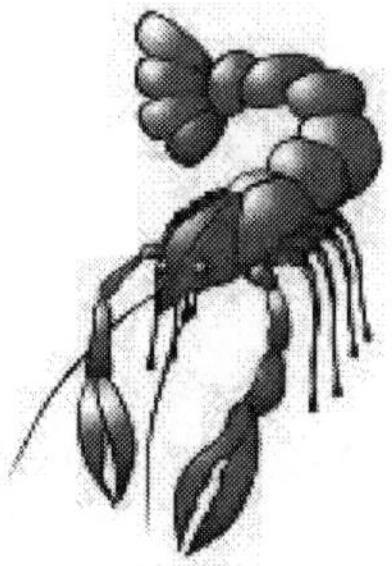

Forward

The vignettes that follow tell, in Cajun dialect, the stories of the wonderful people who populate a piece of Acadiana, in South Louisiana. They are fictions set in the imaginary town of Pigeonaire on the real Bayou *Teche*. The book is in two parts, first the stories of the Acadiana folk, the Cajuns, told in flashes that combined transform the individual stories to a novel about life in the Bayou country. The rest of the book is the recipes, some of which are Cajun and some of which are not.

The Mudbug Tales pay homage to the Cajun people and their wonderful ways. If I fail to depict reality it's because that is not my aim. What I'm trying for is a series of flashes that are lighthearted and present a unique people in an enjoyable way that is worth the read. If I don't get it right it is entirely on me.

The second part of the book is an almost random presentation of recipes for stuff that I like to cook and eat. Some of the recipes are for Cajun style vittles and some are not. The recipes in the book haven't been tested in or by any fancy culinary organization; they are just from my own and my friends' kitchens. We like the dishes that are presented here and hope that you will adapt the recipes to your tastes and enjoy them.

Mudbug, if you don't already know, is a South Louisiana colloquialism for crayfish/crawfish, or écrevisse. They are a true taste treat. Mudbug is also this book's narrator's Cajun nickname.

I've tried to do justice to the Cajun people but I know that it is actually impossible to do so. Cajuns are much too unique for anyone to capture their culture with mere words. So, as way of showing my admiration for the Cajun people I'll just insert my previously published flash piece LOUISIANA. With Louisiana I think you will see my love for that unique State, its Parishes, and its folk and folkways. Here tis:

LOUISIANA

dis ol' boy he hearin' wimmen tawkin' 'bout sumtin' they callin' flash fiction, an' dat get him confuse. dey tourist wimmen, come out onna de porch of the general store carry'n' dey co'colas an' tawkin' high falutin'. Dey be sayin' stuff dis boy ain't never hear befo'. I ask 'em, me, wat dey be talkin' 'bout. Dey say, litrature. a writin' style, dey say, kndna snotty like. me, I doan care no mo' ta unnerstan' what dey be talkin' an tellin' me 'bout so, i ain' lissnen' no mo'. Dat flash fiction juss soun' like showin' off. Flash fiction jess nonesense anyhow, i tink. so, i sip a lil' bit o' whiskey, me, an' i turn to think about sumpin' other than dat flash fiction stuff them wimmen be talkin'. I tink 'bout old times in louisiana. what i maybe unnerstan, some, maybe.

salt smells. crawfish gumbo. écrevisse. sno-cones. roe shrimp. file powder. tur-duk-en. deep fryd. sugar cane.

cottonmouth swimmin'. mississippi. paddle wheeler. atchafalya. spillway gate. pontchartrain. bayou. cajun folk. dancin'.

cherry lips an' a flutterin' eyes. creole lady. cajun queen. flirty-girly. thibadioux. terrebonne. beaux bridge. mulate's. zydaco. mama got a squeeze box. cajun fiddle. new roads. fause rivere.

fish pole. pirogue. parish. cotton bolls. river road. huey long. feliciana. redbone. armadillo. carville. leprosarium. convicts. angola. road gang.

shadows on the teche. evangeline. cypress knees. antebellum. Tabasco® sauce. salt domes. jambalaya. cookin' pot. squirrel stew.

roseate spoonbill inna salt flat. duck flight. fish warden. lafitte skiff. mud flat fingers inna delta. gulf waters. oil rig. alligator. nutria. ducks in vee. pump shotgun. cast net. fishpole. buck knife. cold beer. liv'n off de lan'.

n'orleans. spanish moss. catholics. st louis cathedral. artist stalls. mardigras. octoroon ball. tipitino's. coco & ialya. two sisters. k-paul. whitey's pool room. earl long. blaze in dishabille.

martini gazpacho. étouffée . cafe de monde. galatoire's. doctor john. tchoupitoulas. antoine's. bignet. hurricanes at pat's. sweet honey dripper. fiyo. big easy.

preservation hall. dixieland. barker at the door. marchin' saints. marie le-veau. nevilles chants. voodoo. tombs on top. fevre dream.

louisiana. magic. Wonderland.

lassier les bon temps rouler.

flash fiction? doan know 'bout dat. i ain' hearin' no more o' dat stuff, me.

(a version of LOUISIANA was
previously published in FF Magazine,
Tonya Judy, Publisher)

I have to add a few words to thank the folks who helped with this book.

My wife, MiMi, read the draft ms and provided wise editorial advice. Thanks Darlin'.

Ramon Collins, my good friend, formerly of Bogalousa, LA, now in Boulder NV, published many of the Mudbug Tales in his E-zine, Quiction, Ray also helped with the manuscript.

Others who read the ms and advised me were Lesley Weston, Kat Grosjean, Lloyd Boyd and Wenonah Lyon. These people, friends, are readers extraordinaire who caught my stumbles. I'm eternally grateful for their help.

In the recipe section of the book Rick Stone, Kathy and Kevin Livingston, Johnny Harvey were right there. Francis O'Brien chipped in with Fish and Grits. My son-in-law, Bob Parfitt provided the stuffed mushroom appetizer. I couldn't have done the cooking stuff in this book without any them.

Tabasco sauce is found in several places in this book. The TABASCO® marks, bottle and label designs are registered trademarks and service marks exclusively of McIlhenny Company, Avery Island, Louisiana 70513. www.TABASCO.com.

Mudbug Tales is one hundred percent a work of fiction and any resemblance to anyone, living or dead, is pure coincidence. For any flaws or errors blame me, no one else.

So, here are the stories and the recipes. I hope both please you.

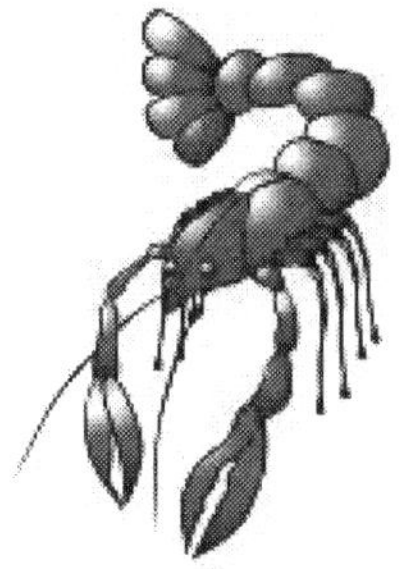

CHAPTER ONE:
Beginnin' Da Tales

Da Cajun Life

Cajun life is hard work and hard play. Getting' down to it dat's da way. Knowin' da time time o' day. Sunup hours fo' da' toilin'. Sundown hours fo' da dancin'. For da kickin' back. Fo' da Cajun repast. O ' course one doan need no sundown on da weekend. Then it's all play, all day.

Usherin' In A New Year

Dere was a blue moon on da Bayou dis New Year's Eve. Dey don't come dat often an' when dey do come dey sometime bring out da looners. We was waitin' an' watchin' fo' trouble in our liddle town o' Pigeonaire but none came. Even da wild Broussard boys behave themself, but dat may be 'cause dey was workin' hard to impress a coupla ladies las' nite.

Anyhoo, we had us a big ol' party down to Dupree's roadhouse. Had a *Zydeco* band wit' fiddles and 'ccordians an' washboards an stuff. All da pretty girlies dance up a storm, shakin' booties, flirtin' wit' da fellas. We hoot an' holler like good ol' Bayou boys do. Da girls seem to get a kick outta dat. Da ol' ladies turnin' up dey noses. Da old men playin' cards --*bourré.* Da *bebes* sleepin' thru it all.

We tossed back a lotta col' ones (Bayou Champagne) an' come da stroke o' midnight we kissed all da ladies.

We had a fine new year party an' we'd jus' like to say *bon annee* to all o' you folk ain' so lucky as to live in Bayou country.

Mornin' Come

New Years day is here on Bayou *Teche* and we all kinda lazy from all da partyin' las' night. Some say it's stretchin' a bit to say lazy. Hung ova is mo' like it dey say. I doan rightly agree. We Cajun folk can hol' our drink an' do fine da nex' day.

Juss a liddle lazy, dat's all.

Fo' Luck an' Fo' Money

Da whole gang goin' back on ova to Dupree's place dis evenin'. Rene, Dupree's olda brudder, da chef, is cookin' up black eye peas wit' rice an' cabbage fo' luck an' money in da new year. Gotta shake on a lot o' peppa vinegar on it to get dat stuff down, but I can sure use some o' dat money.

Gonna have a nice evenin' though. Drink some col' ones. Dance some mo' wit' da pretty girls. Go home early fo' da shuteye.

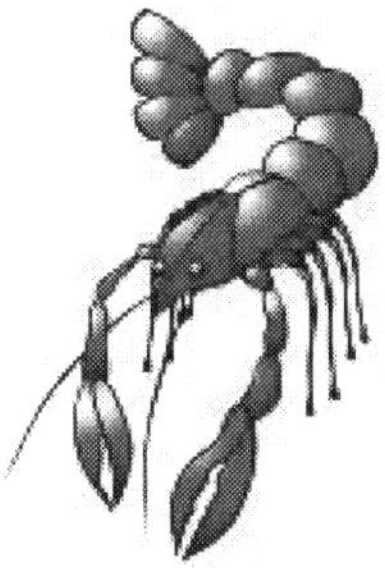

CHAPTER TWO:
Dupree's Roadhouse

Days Is Getting' Longer

I always like da turn of new year. Means days is getting' longer an' springtime ain' long off. Spanish moss takin' on a silvery patina. Marsh grasses startin' to green up. Buds on da sweet gum trees is getting fat and turnin' deep red. Soon dere will be new green leaves.

Dem hyacinths soon be blossomin' on da Bayou waters. Fish will be jumpin'. Fat frogs will be ready fo' giggin'.

Springtime a-coming an' da lazy days o' summa ain' far behind. Always nice when da turn o' da year come, even' da gators seem to be smilin'.

Spring Sprang

Maybe I gotta take back some of what I say 'bout springtime an summa. Spring sprang again an' despite our looking forward to warmer weatha, we ain' singin' like da birdies. No siree, summa comin' on fast an' da hurricane season is 'bout to start up again. Da cleanup o' last year's mess ain' near done yet.

Doan know what gonna happen' to us Bayou folk we get hit 'gain dis year. I keep tellin' myself dat worry is a waste o' time.

But takin' my own advice an' puttin' dat worry away is a whole nudder matta. I can't do her.

An' dat's da troof.

Dupree's Place

Been sittin' here in Dupree's roadhouse fo' a while now listen' to ol' Hank on da jukebox. Tinkin' 'bout da weatha and what could come. Waitin' to see if Marie is comin' in.

Deres a empty beer bottle on da table.

Dat Marie is a pure beauty. She come in we could dance to some o' dem country ballads for a bit. Hank Williams, Willie, Waylon, Jo-El Sonnier, Eddie Raven, George and Tami maybe. Den we can maybe slip out to my cabin on the *Teche*. It sure nice back there on da water.

Coax Marie inta da cabin bedroom, do some snugglin', and then like ol' Hank sung an' I'm quotin' *~son of a gun we have big fun on da Bayou.*

Dat's what I'm dreamin', me.

Gettin' Late

Marie ain' showed up an' now dere's six dead soldiers on da table. I signal Dupree that I'll have a nudder col' one. Ain' nuttin' else gonna happen tonite. Besides I can walk home, so dere's no worry 'bout dat drinkin' an' drivin' stuff.

Stayin' Put, Me

I'm watchin da TV folk an' da announcer say dey's bad stuff happenin' all ova da worl'. Fellas is blowin' folks up, wars is bustin' out, people is gettin' themselfs kidnapped by terrorists. All kinds o' bad tings.

Lemme me tell you, I'm stayin' right here in da Bayou country, me.

Travel 'bout in my skiff an' my pick-em-up truck.
Fish fo' da *sac-a-lait.*
Trow da cast net fo' da shrimps.

Eat fry fish wit' red beans an' rice, an' odder Cajun goodies.
Drink a coupla' col' ones down to Dupree's place.
Listen to dat Zydeco music wit da accordion and da washboard an' fiddle.
Make some fine love wit' a liddle honey bun.

Dat's sure 'nuff da life dat suits me. An' I doan have to get on no airplane, no.

Writin' Onna Wall

I'm standin' front o' da trough in Duprees' men's room, me. Man doan buy beer, he rent it. Me, I 'bout to give up the lease on dem seven col' ones I juss pour down my neck.

Dere's writin' onna wall. I squint, me. Writin' sayin' sumptin' like:

MRDUCS
MRNODDUCS
OSAR CMWANGS
LIB MRDUCS

Dat writin's a puzzle I sure cain figger. An' dat writin' ain' been signed by no one, neither. Muss be wrote by dat smart alec Cajun fellow, Mr. A. Nonny Mouse.

Back at da bar I swallow a bit mo' col' beer. Now I got dat puzzle figure out, I guarantee. Da puzzle sayin'.

Them are ducks.
Them are not ducks.
Oh yes they are. See them wings?
Well I'll be. Them are ducks.

Buncha col' ones are good for stirrin' dat ol' grey matter. Dat's what I say, me.

Could-might be time to get on home now. Might-could be.

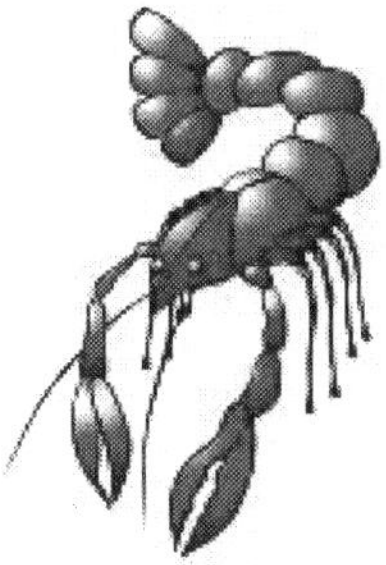

CHAPTER THREE:
Some Bayou Tings

Da Chiren

Bayou chiren from da time dat dey is born are included in da Cajun life. Fo' 'zample, the Cajun folk love to party and dey is 'specially fond o' da *fais do-do*. *Fais do-do* mean a Cajun dance party where da wimmens bring da liddle chiren an' get dem to go to go to sleep, quick like. Story has it dat da wimmen folk want da bebes to go to sleep soon as possible so dat dey make sure dat da husbands ain' dancin' wit' none o' da pretty single gals.

When da chiren get a little olda dey join in on all kinds o' Cajun tings. Dey learn how to hunt an' fish. Dey learn how to cook the Cajun vittles. Dey learn da music, playin' da fiddle, da 'ccordian, da washboard. Dey do da spoonin' at da Cajun picnics an' parties.

Da chiren grow up to honor da ways o' dere ancestors, includin' dere *Mamans* and *Papoots* an' da *Gran-meres* an' *Gran-peres*. Da old folk love da chiren growin' up like dat, 'cause dat's da Cajun way.

One ting for sure 'bout da Cajun folk is dat dey love da chiren. Dem young uns bring pleasure and da smiles to the olda folks faces. Dere ain no question dat chiren are at da heart o' Cajun life

Livin' Off Da Lan'

Cajuns in Sout' Louisiana trace dere roots to da Acadian settlers chased out o' Nova Scotia an' parts o' eastern Quebec an' Maine during French and English contratemps back 'round da middle o' da seventeen-hunnrets. Da settlers didn't have no money an' dey had to find ways to make do.

Dat dey did.

Livin' off da lan' is da Cajun way since our folks firs' come to Acadiana as we like to call da Bayou country. An' da Cajun culture come to have it's own kind of food an' music an' folkways.

Cajuns even come up wit' dere own way o' speakin. Dey use a whole lot of French wit' some English trown in fo' good measure.

Today some o' da younger Cajuns ain' livin' da old ways but dey ain' completely give 'em up either. The Cajun cookin' ain' neva goin' away. Da partyin' at da *fais do-do* still a big part of da culture. Da music still use da fiddles an' accordians an' da washboard. *Bourré* still a popular way o' playin cards. Respec' fo' da old folk is still strong. An' neighbors takin' care o' neighbors an' da neighbors chiren ain' never goin' away.

I tink da best parts o' da Cajun culture will always be here in Sout' Louisiana. Dat's what I hope, anyhoo.

Cast Net

Young 'uns livin' in da Bayou country all have da cast net for catching da shrimps. Doan matter none whetha da chile is a girl or a boy. Come around da sixth birthday she or he gets da first cast net. Starter net is four feet in diameter and as da kid grows so does da net. Big nets is eight feet.

Da nets all have lead weights sewn in around da bottom edge an lines for da throwin' and an' for closin' da net an' retreivin' da catch.

Dere's art to trowin' da cast net. Firs' da net is picked up by da lines so dat it's a straight package an' da line is slipped ova da wrist. Den one o' da weights is picked up and held in da mout' by da teeth. Da net caster put her or his back to da water and wit' a turnin' motion trows da net. Da technique is a lot like swingin' da golf club or a baseball bat. One doan want to forget to open da mouth or one could-might lose a tooth.

If da net is tossed proper it will blossom our an' hit da water full circle. Da weights sink da net ova da swimming shrimps. Den it's pull up on da line an' da net closes an' traps da shrimp. A good cast brings up a dozen or more shrimps.

Kids learn quick to trow da liddle shrimps back in da wata fo' to grow more an' to put da big shrimps in da bucket fo' bringin' home.

Lots of Bayou kids also have da bait lines an' dip nets for catching da blue crabs and da wire-cloth traps for catchin' da mudbugs (dat's crawfish or *écrevisse* for dem dat doan know).

Growin' up on da Bayou is *le bon temps*. Dat's what I tink, me.

Rosate Spoonbill

You get way down sout' in Louisiana where gulf o' Mexico stretch out 'longside da roads goin' toward Texas you could-might see a flock o' dem bird. Roseate Spoonbill is what I'm talkin' 'bout. Dere ain' hardly a prettier sight than dose big pink birds in flight.

Dem pink birds was allas found way sout' in da United States, tip of Florida an' along da Louisiana gulf coast. Now dey showin' up where they ain' never been before. My cousin, GC, up in Sout' Carolina says dere's ten o' dose birds come to his yard where it backs to da salt marsh. Dey been comin' fo' da last couple o' years. Those birds don't rightly belong dat far north, but times they are a changin'.

Could-might be dat global warming is pushing dem birds to new places. Might-could be.

Dem Pretty Flower

Maman love dem pretty purple flower an' so do my sista's, girl chirens, Amiee and Desiree. Maman, she keep dem flower in a 'quarium on a shelf in da kitchen.

Dem flowa is water hyacinth an' dey beautiful, I admit, me. But underneath da beauty dem flower is nasty. Clog the Bayou bank to bank an' kill off da fish. Duckweed gets choked out and da ducks go away. Cain't row the pirogue in da Bayou no mo'.

Cain't pull dem hyacinths out but dey grow right back again. Dynamite doan kill 'em.

Now dey usin a pizzen call 2,4-d on dem hyacinth. Doan know what's in dat stuff but it's workin' on dem flower. Gets me to wonderin' what's gonna happen to Cajun folk dat eat da fish and da ducks got da pizzen in 'em.

I doan know, me, but let me tell you I worry, I guarantee.

Nite Sky

Sometimes I take da *pirouge* out on da *Teche* in da dark o' da nite. It's quiet out dere an' a boy can relax an' do some tinkin'. Annuder ting 'bout bein' alone out dere is lookin' to da stars. Lights in da town mak' in near impossible to see da beauty o' da stars in da nite sky.

Out on da Bayou, away from da town, da sky is a wonda. Stars light up like da jewels in a queen's crown. At da rite time o' da month da moon is spotlightin' on da wata an' turns it to gold an' platinum. Da nite sky mor' beautiful dan da prettiest Cajun gal in alla da sout' Louisiana parishes put together.

When I'm alone out dere on da Bayou dat's da stuff I'm thinking, me. It's amazin', da beauty.

Sugarcane

Cain't hardly tell no story o' da Cajun folk without mentionin' da sugar cane. Cane is big bidness in Louisiana an' a lotta folk make their livin' growin' an' harvestin' an' refinin' dat cane. Dey say dat a half a million folk mak' their livin' one way or da other in da sugar bidness. Dat's a impressive numba.

One o' da tings I always look forward to is da suga cane festival in New Iberia. Dere's carnival rides, a *fais do-do*, street dancin', an' da crownin' o' da sugar queen, sure to be a fine young Cajun beauty.

Dat New Iberia harvest festival is one sweet time.

Da Po'-boy Sammich

Toilin' hard like we Cajuns do can sure work up a man's appetite. Dat's where da Po-boy sammich come in.

Dat Po' Boy sammich is a Louisiana treat on French bread. You can get da sammich naked or dressed. Dressed is wit' da lettuce an' tomato, an' onion, maynez, an' odder stuff. Naked ain't.

Po'-boys come in all manner o' different ways. Dere's da oyster Po' -boy, da shrimp, da col' meat, da roast beast an' ham wit' debris. Po'-boy can be made wit' juss 'bout anyting, even 'gator tail.

Me, I fava dat roast beast an' ham wit da debris.

Wha's dat debris you ask? Debris is da gravy loaded wit' bits of beef dat results from da slow roastin' It's scrumptious-delish, dat's what it is.

Sometimes, I like other Po-boy sammiches. I could-might go fo' da oysta Po-boy dis noon. Dat's what my mouf' is waterin' fo' today, uh-huh.

Fishcamp

Sometimes me an' my good buds like to get away fo' awhile wit-out da wimmen folk. Dat's when we go to da fishcamp on *la Fausse Riviere* up in *Pointe Coupée* Parish.

La Fausse Riviere is an oxbow was years ago cut off from da Mississippi after one o' da bad storms dat shifted da mighty river's course. Now it's a quiet lake wit' Cypress cabins built out ova da water.

When we go to da camp we spend our time drinkin' col' ones, tellin' lies, playing cards, kickin' back an' watchin' sports on da big screen TV. Dang liddle fishin' gets done.

But dat's okay 'cause Louis LeBatt run a grocery store in New Roads juss a few minutes from da camp. He carry fresh fish, shrimps, oysta, an' crabs. His steaks an' pork chops is da best. He got fresh farm veggies. An' he has a big ol' coola full of col' ones.

Louis's grocery is all dat we boys need. Dat's fo' sure.

Da Dipper Ducks

Drive your pick-em-up truck mos' anywhere in sout' Louisiana you gonna see da dipper ducks bobbin' dey haids. They pumps, bring up dat black gold from 'neath da earth. They goin' twenty-four seven.

Lots o' da boys work in da oil patch. Some on terra firma, some out on da rigs in da gulf. Roughneck an' roustabout boys work hard an' their pay is good. Dey can feed their fambilies, educate da chirens, an' still have 'nough money to tow nice boats behind a super pick-up, like da Ford 350 Dually.

Da fac' dat lotsa Louisiana boys work wit da oil is why dey skeptics when it come to know-nuttin' envriomental opinions.

Not dat da Louisiana boys doan understand an' appreciate dat da lan' is fragile an' needin' protection. Dey know dat regulations for keeping tings hunky-dory gotta be, but dem regulations also gotta be writ an' enforced so as not to choke da industry. Goose dat lay da golden egg an all dat.

Makin' da oil patch companies behave is good but dere's trade offs. Dat's all I'm sayin', me.

Mudbugs and Dixie Beer

Dere ain' nuttin' quite so good as a col' Dixie longneck an' a pile o' boil mudbugs afta a hard days carpenterin'. Get home from work. Clean up, put on a fresh pair of Levis an' a clean tee shirt. Hie on down to Dupree's roadhouse. Dance wit' da pretty girls. Swap stories wit' da guys. Try a few hands o' *Bourré*.

Top alla dat good stuff off with a a super mudbug suppa. Spice dem mudbugs wit' a little Tabasco sauce, eat da tails, suck da heads. Have anudder col' Dixie longneck.

Dat is livin' da good life, surely is.

Dem Alligators

Da Bayous in Cajun country is full o' alligators, especially in da swampy areas. Usta was dem 'gators was a dwindlin' 'dangered species an' protected under da law. Not no mo'.

Dem conservation laws gave da 'gator time to come back, an' hoo-boy did dey do dat. Now dey all ova da place an' becomin' a nusance when people live near da wata.

TT Fontenot, one o' my buddies, an' his cousins got dem 'gator tags from da Fish an' Wildlife department an' dey legal 'gator hunters now. Dem boys is makin' good money sellin' da 'gator hides an' da meat. Dey want to get on dat Swamp People TV show dat's on da History channel. A good ting is dat TT always save some o' da 'gator tail meat for da parties we have down to Dupree's place.

Yum, charcoal grilled 'gator tail is 'bout da bes' o' some good eatin'.

Da Bull Gator Story

Roaaaaaaar!

Wha's dat?

It's da sound of spring. Bull 'Gator talkin' to the ladies. All tir'teen feet and fo'teen hundred pounds o' that bad boy is hollerin' --get your tails over here ladies, it's springtime.

Roaaaaaaaar!

Da lady 'gators slip from der dens and swim the pond looking der prettiest, mos' enticing. Several six footers, an eight footer an', hot dang, a ten foot mama covered with moss and mud. Mmmmm-Mmmmm, the Pamela Anderson o' da 'gators. Man, juss look at her rough hide and snaggle tooths.

Bull 'Gator swims over to where she lies at the pond's edge.

A young male 'gator spots Pamela at 'bout the same time as Bull. The young one comes toward her from 'cross da pond.

Roaaaaaaaar!

Dat young 'gator keep a-comin'. A mistake.

Bull , like a torpedo, meets dat boy in the middle o' da pond. Bull snaps his jaw down on the young 'gator's shoulder. The young male thrashes wildly attemptin' to free himself from Bull's jaws. Wata erupts in a white froth that turns pink. The thrashin' goes on for a quarter of an hour. Finally, the young male, now three legged, swims away from Bull.

Bull spits out gristle and hide. He smiles da gator smile.

Roaaaaaaaar!

Bull moves on to Pamela.

~now, springtime alligator sex is much like da fight described above, so, like a propa Cajun fella taught manners by his *Maman*, dis boy will simply say ~Bull and Pamela done the deed.

***

Late autumn come.

A great blue heron settles at the edge of the pond intent on a minnow breakfast. Da bird stares at da water. Patience will, as always, bring rewards. Suddenly, da wata erupts.

Bull 'Gator launches like a rocket from below the surface. Feathas fly. The great blue ain't no more.

Bull 'Gator with the heron's carcass clamped between his teeth slides back into the wata. He'll stuff dat bird, feathas, flesh and bones, in da hole with the remains of a ripenin' deer and go back to his den. Winter coming on and its time to lay up comestibles.

Bull's year was good. Tore a leg off a rival. Nailed Pamela. Watched her incubate the eggs. Witnessed the birth of her brood. Ate ten of Pamela’s twelve hatchlings.

The only down part of Bull's year was da fightin’ mad Pamela biting out a chunk o’ his tail. But, what the heck, dat healed.

Yes Sir, Bull had him a very good year.

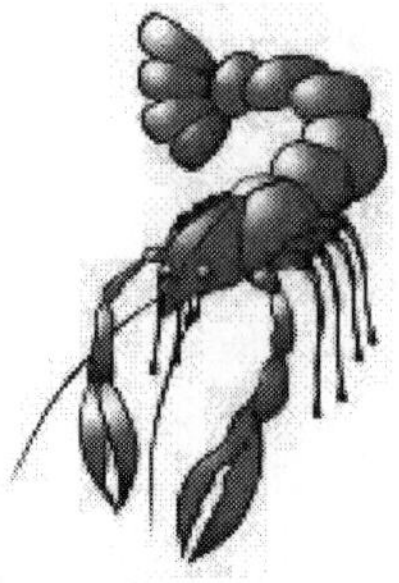

CHAPTER FOUR:
A Liddle Trouble

Dupree's Old'a Brudder

Dupree's old'a brudder, Rene, is 'bout da crankiest guy on da *Teche*. Dat's what I say, me. But, dat Rene sure a fine-good cook. Trow stuff togetha make a man's mout' water. We all put up wit him for dat gumbo wit' chicken and andouille sausage he make, an' da dirty rice, an' da fry fish.

Yup, dat Rene make some succulent morsel. Ain' nuttin' dat man can't cook. Too dang bad 'bout his sour ol' personality.

Dat's what I say, me.

Êtes Vous Ce Que Vous Mangez

Cranky ol' Rene says *Êtes vous ce que vous mangez* is da Cajun way to say you are what you eat. An' here in da Bayou country we all eat good. Especially down to Dupree's when Rene is doin' da cookin'.

Most o' our vittles come from da lan' an' da wata.

We mak' da stews from raccoon, squirrel, nutria an' from some o' da bigger critters like da deer. We use da ducks an' da geese an' some o' da otha birds o' da air. Some backyard chickens too.

Dere's fish, an' shrimp, an' oystas, an' blue crabs, not to mention da *écrevisse*. Sometimes we grill 'gator tail.

Onions, bell peppa, celery (da trinity) an' taters, maters, an sweet corn come from da farms an' da *Maman*'s gardens. We cook a lot with beans an' rice, an' fiel' peas, an' greens.

We like roastin' da whole hog, but when dat ain' possible we smoke a Boston butt or two.

We love big ribeye steaks on da charcoal grill.

So, *Êtes vous ce que vous mangez* is a fact of life. An' we manage dat fact with da best eatin' on da planet earth.

Tabasco® brand pepper sauce

Lotsa folk tink dat Cajun cookin' is firey hot but dat ain' so. Mos' jambalya or *étouffée* or gumbo or red beans an' rice have a good spicy taste but dey ain't 'specially hot.

Dupree's brudder Rene, da chef, know dat da Cajun style cookin' ain' supposed to burn da tongue an' he leave da condiment, mos' 'specially da Tabasco sauce to da customer.

Dat Tabasco sauce is a hot peppa sauce made on Avery Island in Louisiana an' it's da best an' most needed condiment on da table. Cajun folk know hot spice dat's one man's taste can be another man's pizzen. Dat's why da hot peppa condiment an' how much to use is always up to da person doin' da eatin'.

Me, I like a drop or two o' dat Tabasco sauce on mos' of my vittles. Not too much, not too little.

Suppa At Dupree's Place

Dat Rene a bad one. You know who I talkin' 'bout. Dupree's brudder, dat who.

Rene, he heard I called him cranky. I tink it was dat TT Fontenot what tol' him. I'm gonna fix dat liddle blabber mout'. But firs' lemmee say what dat Rene done to me.

I come into Dupree's place 'bout seven las' night, me. Chalkboard say Chicken Fry steak wit' mash taters, butta bean, corn, an' biscuits. Dat's yum food and I order me up a plateful.

What come out o' Rene's kitchen look great. Big steak, pile o' mash all soak in lard gravy, and da veg. Big flaky biscuits onna side.

Trouble was when I try to cut my steak it come to be breaded, deep fry corrugated cardboard.

Yep, dat Rene staple up a couple a pieces a cardboard he cut from a big old' box, bread it up, and fix it for my suppa. He got me good.

Could-might be I deserve wha' I got.

But dat TT gonna get sumptin' from me he ain' neva' gonna forget. Might take a time before I fix him but when I do he gonna be might sorry bout his big mout'. An' dat's a true fac'.

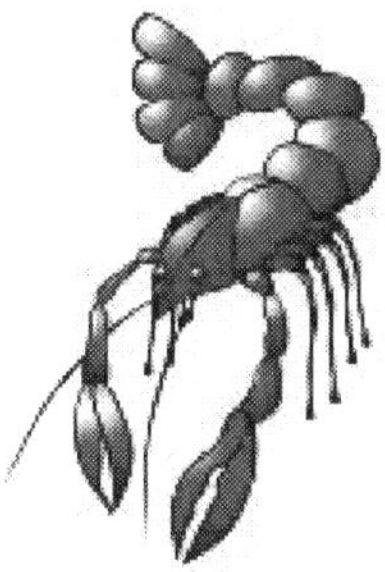

CHAPTER FIVE: Gettin' Even

Fixin' Dat TT

Saddaday comin' an' TT tink he gonna be relaxin'. Dat's what dat boy tink but he got annudder tink comin'. TT gettin' his, is wha' he's gettin'.

TT sayin' he goin' out fishin' for da *sac-a-lait* in da mornin'. An' dat will give me da chance. Bobo Arquette got him a big ol' rubba wata moccasin dat I can borrow. Put dat fake snake in TT's beer cooler.

TT's deathly 'fraid o' snakes. He reach in da cooler for a col' one he likely to have da heart attack. Mo' likely he mess his drawers.

Serve TT right. Him tellin' Dupree's olda brudda dat I claim he's one cranky bassard.

Blabba mout' gonna get his comeuppance.

Da Liddle Girl

Gotta hold off on my fixin' dat TT. Vangie's baby girl, liddle Irene, gone missin' an' findin' her is what's important now. Her momma in a state o' frenzy. Says da chile never wanda off before. But, she's gone.

Dey was in da Superette to get some *Andouille* an' red beans an' Vangie turn her back for a minute an' dat chile juss vanish. Vangie look all ova da store an' she ain' dere.

Vangie go outside an' call da chile's name, real loud like. Dere ain' no answer. Afta a while folk gather an dey start beatin' da bush looking fo' dat baby girl.

Huntin' fo' da Chile

Dere was a whole lotta hours dat da town folk was out beatin' da bushes an' we was all getting' worry. Dat girl chile wasn't being foun' an' we was beginnin' to fear da worse. Da ting dat was so awful was a report o' da prison break come ova da radio. Da boys all got dere shotguns an huntin' rifles an' dey was loaded wit ammo.

Den da break came.

Dupree heard some hummin' comin' from a swamp hummock. He go back dere to investigate an' he foun' da baby girl, liddle Irene. She was playin' wit a nest o' marsh bunnies, hummin' a lullaby to dem baby critters. Seems da chile has da gift o' bein' able to talk wit' da animals.

Anyhoo, Dupree scoop up da liddle girl an' bring her back to her momma. Dat liddle Irene *bebe* cry some as she din't want to leave dem bunny babies behind.

Turn out da 'scaped convict was hidin' in an ol' fish camp shack on da false river an' some boys cauchted him. He is on da way back to Angola right now.

So, da day ended well, an' we all gathered at Dupree's place. Had us some col' ones an' some fry catfish an' dirty rice.

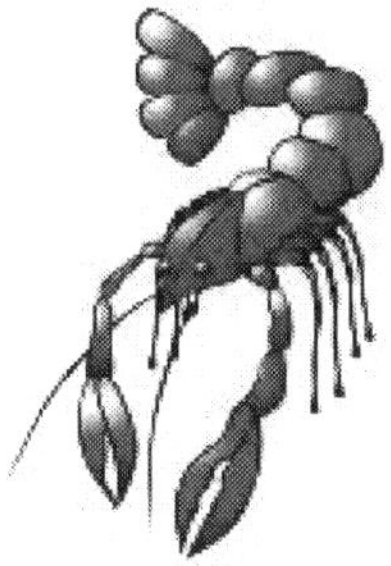

CHAPTER SIX:
Now I Gone An Done It

Horseplay An' Da Horsepistol

Oh-oh, now I done gone an' done it. TT's in da horsepistol caus' o' my horseplay wid da rubba water moccasin. He was reachin' in da cooler fo' a col' one when he saw dat fake snake.

Dat did it.

Ol' man Broussard was fishin' off da bridge near to Dupree's roadhouse and he say TT scream and stan' bolt upright in da skiff. Skiff rock an TT get trow out an whack his haid onna live oak root on da creek bank.

Makin' matters worse TT's a crawlin' out o' da wata an' a big ol' coppahead bite him on da hinder.

After ol' man Broussard got done laughin' his fool head off he go down to da verge and pull TT from da mud at da wata's edge to da dry lan'. Trow dat boy in da back o' his pickup and haul him to da 'mergency room. TT had to have his hinder cut an' da pizzen pumped outta him.

Dat boy gonna be allright in a coupl'a days but I'm feelin' bad, me. Prolly gonna have to go to da church dis afta-noon and 'fess my sins to Fadda LeBlanc.

Dat TT, sometime I tink he's mo' botha dan he worth. An' dat's a fac'.

Marie Got Her Nose In Da Air

Life is flat out miserable in da Bayou country dese days. Da prettiest gal in Sain' Martin parish actin' like I ain' alive. Ever since I put dat rubba snake in da coola an TT ended up in da horsepistol Marie been snubbin' me. I forgot dat Marie is TT's younger sista and dat forgettin' is costin' me dear.

I call Marie on da cell phone an' she hang up. I see her on da street an' she cross to da odder side. Yesstidday I find my high school ring in da mailbox. No note with dat ring, no nuttin'.

Gonna have to eat me some humble pie an' make up wit TT. Mabee pay fo' da boy's beers at Dupree's place next Friday nite. Maybe hep him fix up dat ol' ElCamino dat's rustin' in his *Maman*'s yard.

Gotta get dat TT on my side so's he put in da good word to Marie. Cain't stan' Marie snubbin' me alla time. Gonna have ta tink o' sumptin'.

Plannin' On Da Party

Gonna mak' tings good again on da Bayou. Sadaday I'm plannin' to sponsor a *fais do-do* ova to Dupree's roadhouse on da *Teche*. Invite da whole crowd dat hang out at da roadhouse, but especially TT an' Rene, an' dat sweet Marie. Make up fo' da trouble I cause.

Gonna cook up fry fish an' also boil da mudbug an' cook some chicken an' sausage gumbo. Havin' alla da fixin' -- dirty rice, cole slaw, butta corn, slice 'maters, pickle an' onion an all kinds peppas and peppa sauce. Buncha corn bread. Col' beer an' wine.

Gonna have da band with da guitar da fiddle da washboard da drums an' da 'ccordion. All da Cajun music, specially dat Jolie Blon'.

We gonna party it up an' all be friends again. Gonna make bygones be bygones. Makin' sure dat me an da lovely Marie is hook up again.

Dat's da plan.

Fais Do-Do

Las' nite we had da *fais do-do* down to Dupree's place on da Bayou. Whole town turn out fo' a fried *sac-a-lait* treat wit alla da fixin's. Lots an lots o' scrumptious vittles, washed down, of course, wit' beaucoup col' ones.

We had us a time.

Almos' Worked Out

Dat *fais-do-do* almos' work out fo' me. Prit near. Almos'. Not quite.

Da whole gang was ova' to Dupree's roadhouse, eatin' da food an' drinkin' da wine an' da beer. Dancin' to da *Zydeco*. We was all feelin' good an' we was all freinds again. Pretty Marie was dancin' wit me, nuzzlin' close, sayin' sweet nuttins in my ear. Da nite was goin' good. Tings was hunky-dory.

Den wham-bam, all da debbil break loose.

Da Broussard brothers, Herve an' K-Paul, was tipsy an' dey found a ol' croquet set in da back lot shed. Dey took to smashin' dem wood balls 'round da field. One o' dem flyin' balls whack Marie smack inna ankle.

Now Marie is in da horsepistol wit a cast up to her knee. She madder than a stirred up scorpion an' she ain' speakin' to me.

Dang ol' Broussards. They done da ugly deed an' I get da blame, me. Man can't win nohow.

Doan know what I'm gonna do now. Gotta tink o' sumptin'.

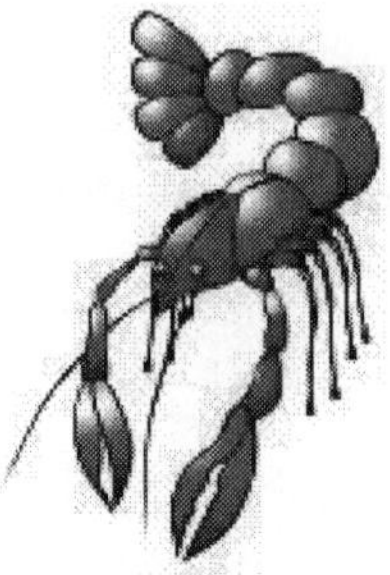

CHAPTER SEVEN: Wicked Wimmens

Ain' No Secrets

Dere ain' no secrets in da Bayou country. Somebody tell somebody else sumptin' an' it get tole all around. Dat happened an' Dupree's place is a buzzin'. Pretty soon everybody know what's what. An' da secret comin' out is wha' done save me.

Here's what come down.

Marie, she in da horsepistol wit da broke ankle an she figurin' sympathy get her what she want. So she tell TT she ain' really mad wit me. She playin' on my sympathy. Say she don't wan't to keep my high school ring no mo', but that's cause she want it replaced. She figurin' she can wheedle me inta buyin' da diamond 'gagement ring. Tinks I want her dat bad.

Da word go aroun' Dupree's bar 'bout what Marie is schemin' an' dat word circle 'round an' get back to me. TT tole a buncha folk what Marie say. Dupree hear an' he tol' me.

Turns out dem Broussard boys causin' da accident ain' hurt me at-tall. In fac' dey save my neck by bringin' Marie's true colors out. I tink I owe dem boys a fava. Maybe a coupla col' ones. Dat's what I tink, me.

Now Da Momma's Mad

TT's in da doghouse wit his Momma now. Blabba mout' TT tol' all ova da *Teche* 'bout dat schemin' Marie tryin' ta get me hitched to her an' dat word get back to me. I dump dat Marie flat.

Trouble is Marie's Momma (same woman is TT's Momma too) was plannin' on getting dat gal outta her house, offa her payroll so to speak, an' onto mine.

TT mess wit' da Momma's plan good.

TT's Momma awful mad at him. Marie mad at him. TT down in da dumps.

Gonna have to buy da boy a col' one tonite at Dupree's Dat'll perk his flaggin' spirit.

Dat's fo' sure.

Da Big Lie

Marie's Momma goin' all ova da parish tellin' anybody wha' will lissen' dat I dump her daughta' fo' no reason. Marie tellin' dat story too. Dat's calumny, dat's what dat is. Folks got half a brain know da troof. Sure I dump Marie but dat ain' no way near to da whole story.

Marie an' her Momma, dey was tryin' ta back me inna corner. Dey both know dat.

But, dem wimmens' plan backfire. Ain' no way I was eva gonna buy no 'gagement ring fo' dat Marie. Gal's pretty, got a nice booty she shake onna dance floor. I enjoyed bein' hook up wit' her some. But she is a schemer. An' she always like to fool aroun' wit all o' da odder boys. Ain' no way to trust her fo' da long haul.

Ain' no neva-mind 'bout Marie's schemin' an' foolin''round, dem lies 'bout me dumpin' her wit' no reason is goin' 'roun. I'm gonna have to spen' all my time defendin' my honor.

Dat Dupree betta have a lot o' col' beer on ice. Gettin' my name clear is gonna take a while. Dat's fo' sure.

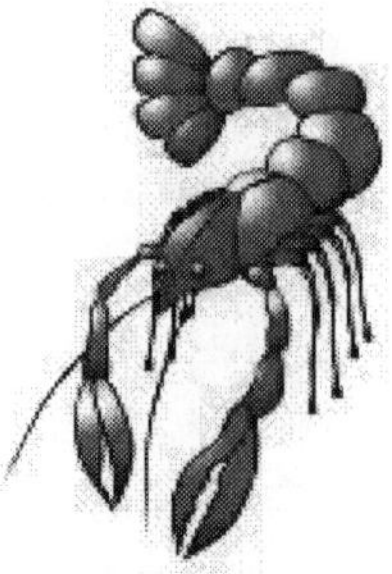

CHAPTER EIGHT:
Gettin' Out From Under

Eureka!

I was sittin' in Dupree's place sippin' on a col' one when it come to me. Bang, juss like dat, da solution to my problem.

Fix up Marie's mudda, Desiree, wit Dupree's olda brudder Rene and fix up Marie wit one o' dem Broussard boys. Doan matta which Broussard, Herve or K-Paul, dey cut from da same mold. Fun lovin', dat's what dem Broussards be.

Dupree agreed wit me.

Dupree says Marie's Momma, Desiree, might get da sour puss offa Rene's mugg. An' he say he could see how one o' dem fun luvin' Broussards could-might distract Marie.

So we went to work aroun' da town talkin' up da get togethas.

We was da Cajun Cupids.

Took us 'bout two weeks but it worked. Marie an' her Momma both hooked up. Ain' nobody on my case no mo'. An' it lookin' like we gonna have some weddin's here in da Bayou country.

Yep, we gonna have big fun.

One Weddin' An' Four Funeral

Dere was rejoicing here on da Bayou but it din't las' long before dere was big sadness.

Marie's Mudda , ol' Desiree, marry Dupree's olda brudder Rene. Dat cranky bassard even smile when he kiss da bride. Den we all walk from da church ova to Dupree's place fo' da *fête*.

Dat's when da bad ting happen.

Dupree's place has a big ol' back gallerie built out ova da Bayou. We was all out dere on dat gallerie eatin' da weddin' food an' drinkin' an' dancin' when da dang thing collapse. Seems dat category four hurricane dat come tru here a while back weaken da timbers.

Da whole buncha us tumble into da Bayou. We all good swimmas an' it woulda been allright but for da 'gators an' da snakes.

A 'gator got Rene thereby makin Desiree a widow fo' da fourth time. An' da moccisans got bot' o' da Broussard brothers an' da snakes dey got TT too.

Awful lot o' tragedy fo' one small community to bear. One weddin' an' four funeral. We gonna bring a jazz band up from N'awlns to give Rene an' da Broussards an' TT a proper Bayou country sendoff.

Den we gonna get togetha an' fix Dupree's gallerie. Dat's what we gonna do. Get busy so's da saddness doan ovawhelm us.

Cause life gotta go on. Dat's fo' sure.

Wake Up Sweatin', Me

Dat stuff 'bout da gallerie porch fallin' in da Bayou was so vivid it 'bout scare da pajamas offa me. Technicola, dat's wha' it was.

Whole buncha folk screamin' an' swimmin fo' dry lan'. Rene, Dupree's olda brudder, TT an' da Broussard boys not makin' it, getting' kilt by dat' snapping 'gator an' dem nasty snakes.

Hoo-boy, it all seem so real. I woke up sweatin' from dat nightmare. Tinkin' it was da troof.

But it ain' what happened at all, an' evra-ting is allright now.

Ain' nobody even got hurt much less died. Dat nightmare dream o' mine was all that it was, but it was da worse one ever.

Musta had me one or two many col' ones at da weddin' fête. Musta had.

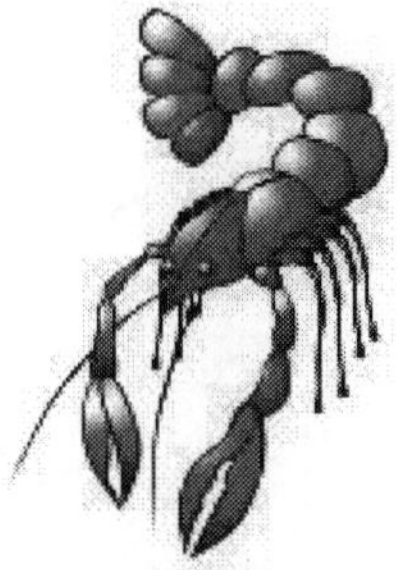

CHAPTER NINE:
Disaster Onna *Teche*

Kickin' Back

Tings is quieted down on da *Teche* an' in our liddle Bayou town o' Pidgeonaire. Rene, Dupree's olda brudder, an' Desiree off on dey honeymoon. Marie an K-Paul Broussard is spoonin'. Me an Dupree are kickin' back an' enjoyin' a coupla col' ones.

Here come TT.

Gotta give dat boy credit. He run off at da mout' 'bout me callin' Rene a cranky bassard. Den he hep' mess tings up wit' me an' Marie (on secon' thought he maybe hep' me out dere).

Anyhoo, TT's big mout' end up wit a both weddin' fo' his Momma an' a buddin' affair for his sista, Marie. Dat's all good. An' now, here TT come big as life. I guess I gotta buy dat boy a coupla col' beers, me.

Suppa Tonite

Rene on his honeymoon so Dupree's cookin' tonite. His special is da Dupree burger wit cucumba, onion, an' 'mater salad.

Here's da recipes. Of course Dupree makin' a big batch fo' all da customas. Dis here is fo' a liddle batch.

For da Dupree burga' use a poun' an a half o' good burgameat --groun' roun'/chuck mixed togetha is da best. Dice up a onion real fine. Add da onion to da meat wit some catsup, an' worchestershire sauce, an some Tabasco sauce. Spice dat mix wit a liddle salt, a lotta fresh groun' black peppa, an' some mixed 'erbs. Squish it all togetha an it'll be da runny mess at dat point. Add juss enough dry bread crumbs or cracka crumbs to firm up dat mess. Shape into four big patties. Broil on da charcoal or da gas grill. Serv' onna toasted bun wit mo' catsup.

To make da cuke, 'mater, an' onion salad Dupree uses:

two ripe maters, diced in kinda larg' pieces
a big onion diced da same
two peel cucumbas sliced
lots o' fresh ground pepper

Pour on da Greek vinaigrette dressing, (or a red wine vinegar an' oil dressing) several ounces (Farmer Boy brand o' Greek derssin' is good). Mix dat stuff all togetha an' put it in da fridge fo' a bit.

Mmmmmmmm. Dupree burgas are fine eatin an dat salad is simple but deelish. Gotta have a col' longneck wit dis meal.

Ol' Dupree almost as good a cook as his olda brudder, Rene. An' dat's a true fac'.

Sno-Cones

Got to tinkin' bout col' refreshment afta a hard day's dusty-dirty work. Dere's roadside stands all tru da Cajun Bayou country where one can get da sno-cone. Dat's shaved ice wit' sweet flavored syrup in a cone shaped Dixie cup.

Sno-cones come an a bunch o' different flavas; cherry, rasberry, orange, lemon, blueberry an' some others.

Some folk say dere's a big difference 'tween da N'Awlins style snoball an' da Cajun sno cone. Dey say in N'Awlins da shaved ice is fine like a soft snow an' da flavas are rich.

The Cajun sno-cone is made wit' a coarser shaved ice an' simple sugary fruit syrups.

Doan matter none dat da Bayou country sno-cone ain' fancy, they mighty good. Wet a workin' man's whistle. Especially after a sweaty day's work at da carpterin' bidness.

Could Be Cajun -- Could Be Creole

Lots of da food dat we Cajun folk cook is whipped up wit' the brown roux an' da trinity (chopped onion, celery, an' green bell peppa). We use a lot of beans and rice. Mos' Cajun dishes are concoctions wit' meat, an' seafood, and fowl. Dat's da Cajun style.

Some folks call dat food Creole, but that ain't rightly so unless 'maters are used in da recipes. Annuder difference 'tween Cajun an' Creole cookin' is in da roux. Cajun roux is made wit' lard or oil an' flour, Creole roux uses butta.

Both da Cajun and da Creole cooks like makin' da gumbo an' dat may be da root of da confusion 'bout da two different ways of cookin' stuff. Da Cajun an' Creole gumbos are both delicious but dey are different. Cajun gumbo is made wit' a brown roux base and is thick like a stew an' da Cajun gumbo doan have no 'maters. Creole style gumbo has da tomatoes and is mo' like a soup than a stew.

Doan matter none if da cookin' is Cajun or Creole, it's all good eatin'. An' dat's da troof.

Nearin' Day's End

Past midnite on da Bayou and da stars is shining bright, reflectin' off da wata'. Dere's a cresent moon in da sky. Ain' no noise. Da' egrets an' da herons gone to bed an' their squawkin' fights ova minnows ain' to be heard no mo' tonight.

Me an' Dupree an' TT is sittin' here on da gallery sippin' col' ones. Alla Dupree's customa long since been fed an' gone on home.

Dis is da best time fo' buddies. Juss sittin' on da porch tellin' tales. No wimmen folk here to contradic' us. An' we can laugh loud an' burp an' fart all we want to without getting dem nasty looks. Dat's da troof.

Shatterin' Da Quiet

We was still on Dupree's porch when da siren blast off. Loud in da middle o' da quiet night. Da Fire Chief's red Ford Ranger scream past Dupree's place follow by da hook an' ladda and da pumpa truck. All tree o' us, me an' Dupree an' TT, is volunteer fire fighters so we jump inta my pick-em-up an' take off afta dat fire equipmen'.

Get to *Tchapotulas* street an' we find it's Rene's cottage onna *Teche* dat's on fire. Flames is lickin' tru da roof raftas an' comin' outta where da windows usta was. Only ting we can do is make sure da fire doan spread to da odder houses nearby.

Who Done It?

Good ting Rene on his honeymoon. Him an' Desiree is safe. But, we all wonderin' if Rene has da enemy wha' start dat fire. Someone he ain't invite to da weddin', might-could be.

In a while when dat boy Rene get back to Pigeonaire we gonna all get togetha an rebuild da cottage. Den Renee can trow a *fais do-do* to say tanks. Dat's how it's done here in Bayou country.

An' we like it dat way juss fine.

Still, we tinkin' maybe Rene betta invite evera-body he know. Sombody might turn down dat invitation or betta, accept, an' den go skulkin' 'round da *fais do-do*.

Den maybe we got us a suspect. Maybe.

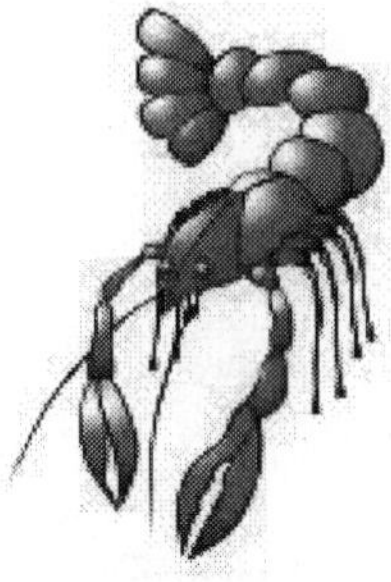

CHAPTER TEN:
Cajun Cooperation

Rebuildin' Rene's Cottage

Rene an' Desiree come back from da honeymoon an' dey was devastated. Desiree been cryin' fo' bout a week now an' Rene stompin' about da town an' yellin' he's gonna cautch da dirty rat what burn his cottage down. Says he gonna wring dat low down-no good's neck.

Da townsfolk is in a hurry to get da rebuildin' done. Dat way we quiet Desiree an' Rene down some. We already started da job o' work.

Firs' ting we do is drive da pilin' fo' gallarie and kitchen section of da cottage. Dem areas is built out ova da Bayou. Da phone company had some surplus creosote poles an' dey donate dem' fo' pilin'. We gonna jet dem pole down inta da Bayou muck an finish dem off by cappen' dem wit da steel hat an' wackin' dem wit da big sledge hammas. Brute work dat is. Gotta stan' in da skiffs to do da pile drivin'.

Da rest o' da cottage is o' terra firma an' doan present no special problem. We got us lotsa brawn an' brain here in Pigeonaire to work da job. We got pick-em-up trucks an' Bobcats, and tractas wit' buckets an' backhoes. We got all kinda tools. Got da compressors an' da nail guns. Got da skill saws an' da powa miter saws an' da sawzalls too. Ain' gonna be no problem wit da rebuildin'.

Da only mishap so fa' is TT whack his tumb wit a hamma an' had to go to da doctor's office. Now he got a big ol' bandage an say he cain't work. Slacka, dat's what I tink, me.

Da lumba yard owned by ol' Antoine Broussard. He's Herve an' K-Paul's *papoot*. He donatin' da buildin' materials. Fadda LeBlanc run a church bazaar an' raise enough money for da plumbin' and lightin' fixtures an' da kitchen appliances.

We makin' progress on da job but speculation 'bout who done da arson getting' thicker dan Spanish moss on da 'vangeline oak over to St. Martinville.

Folks is tinkin' da fire was set by anybody Rene eva had a cross word wit. Dat's everabody an' so dat can't be da troof.

I doan tink we eva gonna caucth da culprit, me. An' it prolly doan matta. Dis new cottage shapin' up to be much betta dan da rickety ol' one what burn down.

Maybe nobody set dat fire. Maybe it was juss worn out ol' wirin'. Dat's prolly it. Time gonna tell wha' da real story gonna be.

Least wise dat's what I tink, me.

Saddaday

Saddaday's here an' da work tools is put up till Monday. Me an' da boys get to kick back an' enjoy. Drink some col' ones, tell some lies, play some cards, dance wit' da pretty girls. Sometimes I feel real bad fo' all o' da married guys what got dem honey-dos on da weekends.

Dem honey-dos is sumptin' makes me think real hard 'bout how good life is da way it is. But then dere's dat pretty redhair librarian from Plaquemines who kinda turns my eye. Yessiree, Marie is busy now wit' K-Paul an' I'm offa da hook. Dat redhead gal from Plaquemines get me to thinkin', yes.

Rumor Causin' Da Trouble

We got da cottage mos' rebuild now. Da final paintin' gonna be done today. Tomorra da tongue an' groove heart pine floors go in. We got dat wood from an' ol' Mississippi riva plantation house dat was bein' tore down. Da Broussard boys lug it to da lumba yard and dey *Papoot* run it tru da millin' machine. Dem flo' board lookin' like new.

Afta da floor go in den dere's nuttin' but da punch list. Finish da paint where necessary, fix a liddle flaw here, fix a liddle problem dere. Dat's all, --an' da cottage is done.

Now da trouble brewin'. Dat TT wit' his sore tumb ain' got nuttin' to do but run his mout'. Somehow he remind Rene 'bout me badmoutin' him an' how mad I got when Rene cook me da corrugated cardboad fo' dinna.

I wasn't mad a-tall, I thought it was funny dat Rene got me so good. But dat ain' how TT tell it. TT remind Rene it's me talkin' how it prolly bad ol' wires started dat blaze. Implyin' I'm tryin' ta cova my tracks, me.

Now Rene lookin' daggas at me. Tinkin' maybe I'm da one wha' burn down his cottage.

Dat's nonsense but dat doan stop Rene's suspicion, especially when Desiree remind him dat we had contratemps ova dat troublemakin' daughta o' hers, Marie.

Da whole town lookin' at me kinda funny dese days.

Dat TT ain' nuttin' but trouble. Da *fais do-do* at Rene's and Desiree's new home is set fo' Sunday evenin'. I'm almost afraid to show up.

Dat ain' da firs' word o' a lie, no.

Nervous Some, me

I been tellin' dis story fo' awhile an' dere ain' none o' you even know my name. It's *Jacques Arvenaux*. But mos' folk 'round here juss call me da Mudbug. Da reason is 'cause I gobble down mo' than my share o' dem critter.

I'm tellin' my name in case tomorrow doan work out. We Cajun folk essentally a peace lovin' lot, but dat doan mean tempas doan sometime flare. An' sometimes bad tings happen, like wit da fish scalin' knives we all carry in sheaths on our belts.

Anyhoo, today Sadaday an' alla da final touches get put to Rene's and Desiree's cottage. I'm a carpenter by trade an' I supervised all da woodwork in da cottage. Maybe some day I'll have my own construction bidness. Meanwhile I make 'nough to keep my belly full and afford my col' ones down to Dupree's place.

Tomorow is da housewarmin', da *fais do-do*.

Rene rememba I call him cranky an' now he tinkin' dat maybe I'm da firebug. I'm a liddle nervous 'bout dat, yes. Doan know 'bout Sunday? Doan know at all.

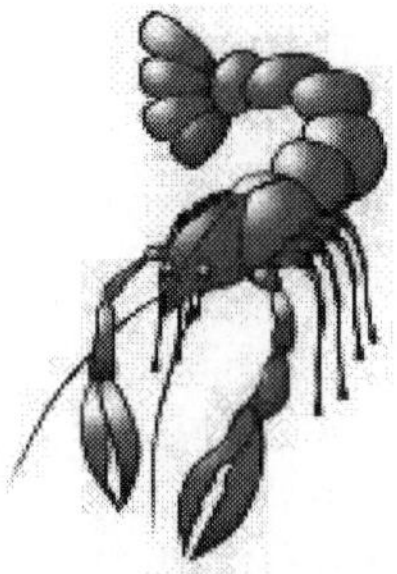

CHAPTER ELEVEN:
Housewarmin' Party

Housewarmin'

Sunday come an' da party was in full swing when I screw up my courage an git dere. Dere's gas cookers in da yard wit' big steel pot on 'em. Dey deep fryin' turkeys, dey boilin' mudbugs, dey cookin' rice an' beans wit da *andouille* sausage. Da wimmen folk all bring side dishes, casseroles, green beans, collards, an' desserts, all kinda pie an' cake an' puddins.

Dere's lotsa cooler wit plenny o' col' beer an' wine on da ice. Haf' da folk already a bit tipsy and da odders is gettin' dere. Dey dancin' an' laughin', tellin' jokes, an' tellin' gossip. Da *Zydeco* ban' playin' *Allons danser Colinda* when I come in.

Frettin'

Been here on 'bout two hour now an' nuttin' bad happen yet. But here come dat Rene wit da scowl on his mugg. He jamb a finger inta my chest an' deman' to know if I'm da culprit. I swat dat finger away an' give dat boy a big ol' shove. All da guests at da party is gatherin' to see wha' gonna happen.

Dupree push his way tru da crowd. He's a big boy dat Dupree, was Louisiana Golden Glove champ when he was younga'. Dupree hear me cussin' Rene out an' he col' cock me. Den, cause he my bes' fren' he slug his brudder Rene who also was swearin'.

Den I hear a scratchin' noise. Rene hear it too. We bot' say 'wha' dat' ' at da same time.

Da Mystery Solved

Dupree hep' us to our feet an' we go outside an' get flashlights from da pick-em-ups. Shine dem lights unda da house crawl space an' dere's eyes shinin' back at us. One o' dem mask bandit up between da floor joists gnawin' on da bran' new 'lectric wires.

Rene an me juss look at each odder an' nod. Was a racoon wha' started da fire an' he tryin' to do 'er again. We shoo da critter away an' go back to da party.

Tomorrow we gonna get da 'lectrician to come back an' put dem wire in critta proof conduit.

Tonite we gonna party. 'cause me an' Rene is frens 'gain. An' dat's a good ting.

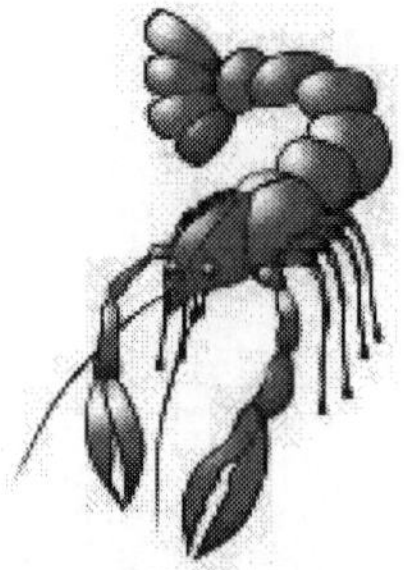

CHAPTER TWELVE:
Da Readhead Gal

When She Let Her Hair Hang Down

Dat librarian down ta da Plaquemine parish library ain' what her home folk tink. She in da library wit her red hair up tight in a bun and wearin' dem fusty clothes an' dem horn rim glasses. Well, le'mee tell you, mos' any Saddaday you can see sumptin' different.

Dat gal, she drive on up ta Mulate's in *Breaux Bridge* where the Plaquemine folk ain't and she can have her a time without no back-bitin' comments an' old ladies tut-tuttin'.

Her flamin' red hair gonna be way down an' her mini skirt gonna be way up. An' she gonna be wearin' one o' dem low cut peasant blouse. She'll be dancin' up a storm to Eddie Raven and Jo-El Sonnier an' dere Cajun tunes.

Dat gal sure a purty sight, I guarantee.

You see her back in Plaquemine you ain' never gonna believe wha' I say. Juss gonna tink I'm tellin' da firs' word o' a lie.

Come on up to Breaux Bridge nex' Saddaday night; see if what I say ain' da honest troof.

Breaux Bridge

Marie and K-Paul took to squabblin' so me an' both a da Broussard boys decided to drive on over to *Breaux Bridge* las' night. Dem Broussard boys struck up an acquaintance wit' a coupla ladies from ova dat way an' thought dey might-could get to know 'em better.

I tol' dem boys I'd ride along but I didn't say a ting 'bout dat sweet redhead gal I been tinkin' 'bout lately. No sirree, I kept my own thoughts to me. Ain' gonna give dem Broussards no ammunition fo' raggin' on me.

Anyways, we get to Mulates's roadhouse an' da lady is dere an' lookin' mighty fine. After a quick col' one I ask her to dance. We out on da floor shakin' booty an' I'm feeling mighty fine.

Den all o' a sudden dis big guy grabs me from behin' and starts shoutin' 'bout me foolin' wit his gal. Dat boy so huge I feel like da boy "wit' da hair colored yella", in dat Lynard Skynard, "gimmee three steps mister" song.

Wouldn't have been so bad but dat redhead gal is laughin' and sayin' we was just dancin' and I doan mean a ting to her.

Da big boy keep yellin' an' I could see dat he wasn't gonna let dis go. So, I rear back an' col' cock him. He lying out col' on da dance floor an da bouncers come an grab me an' rush me out da door. Dat's okay, –out is where I want to be.

Dem Broussards come on outside an' we pile in da pickup an' head fo' home. Now da Broussards is raggin' on me sumptin' fierce an' I know dey gonna let all our friends in on da joke.

Shoulda stayed here in Pigeonaire an' gone ova to Dupree's to dance wit da local gals. Shoulda, 'cause I sure learnt da grass ain' greener.

An' dem Broussards got enough o' da ammunition to give me fits fo' a long while.

Back Home An' Safe

We back in Pigeonaire an' ain' seen hide nor hair o' dat big fellow from *Breaux Bridge*. An' dat's a good ting. Looks to me like da coast is clear.

I gotta say dat goin' on ova to Breaux Bridge done some good. I ain't tinkin' 'bout dat librarian no mo'. Her laughin' an' makin' sport fixed me good. She sure ain' da gal I conjured up in my head. Nope, not a'tall she ain', so, I'm ova da 'fatuation, me.

Here in our little town o' Pigeonaire da local gals are lookin' mighty good to me.

Dat's a true fac'.

Da Town Money

Me, I'll stick aroun' Pigeonaire fo' a bit. Stay ta home an' mind my ps an' my qs. Our liddle town ain' much but we got a gubmint an' I'm da 'lected treasurer dis year.

Dis mornin' I crunched da numbers an' it looks like we got about thirty gran' in da bank an' 'bout seventy gran coming in wit' dis year tax. Da money adds up to ova and 'bove da town's fixed expenses. Dat's a good ting, money da council can use to fix da roads an' da levees. Or, da money can be set aside fo' emergencies, like a hurricane disasta. Or, da town could-might have a blowout of a crawfish boil an' have some change left ova.

Da town fathas gonna argue long an loud when I present dem options, I guarantee.

It's Da Anniversary

Tinkin' 'bout da town money remind me dat it's da anniversary o' dat monsta hurricane Katrina, dat's what. Make me shake rememberin' about dat ol' storm.

Today dere's a new one o' dem tropical depression churnin' 'roun' da Carribean islands, right nex' to dat Sain' Lucia. Dat's what da cutie pie weatha gal on da television sayin'. Sure hope dat depression doan become no hurricane.

Katrina come an' kiss an' hug us one year ago. Wind howled sumptin' awful. Doan wan't it like dat eva 'gain,no.

Dere ain' a one o' us dat ain' scared o' a storm like dat Katrina repeatin'.An' dat's da troof.

Hurricane Season

Dere's some stuff goin' on dat worry me. No, dat ain' right. It's da stuff dat's not goin' on what worry me. Da gulf coast is a mess an' it ain' getting' much betta. My friends in south Mississippi an Alabama is flat out bein' ignored. Da folks in da southern Louisiana parishes doan seem to exist. An' now da hurricane season is come on to us again an' da gubmint ain' done da job needed doin'. Now, I doan tink da gubmint owes folk a livin' but I do tink it do have some responsibility.

Gubmint gotta fix da da roads an da levees an' da bridges an' stuff, dat's what da gubmint gotta do. Folks can't fix dere own places if dere ain' no infrastructure. But it seem da gubmint doan even understan' dat.

Things could be a sight better than dey are, but maybe us Bayou folk juss ain' got no pull up where we need it. Darn shame if that's da case.

Me, I hope it ain' so.

Is Da Ill Wind

Dey say it's a ill wind dat blows no good. Ha! Dem dat says dat nonsense ain' never lived through no hurricane. Hurricane ain' never blow no good, fo' no one, no how.

How-some-ever, bein' as dat is, dis hurricane season ain' throw up any big storms so far. Dem few storms dat did develop stayed out in da 'lantic an' dint make any landfall in Bayou country.

Now, da hurricane season ain' ova yet, an' it ain' no time fo' celebratin' juss yet. Still, me, I'm might-could celebrate a mite and pop a col' one.

Dat's ‘cause I do believe we could-might have dodged da bullet dis year.

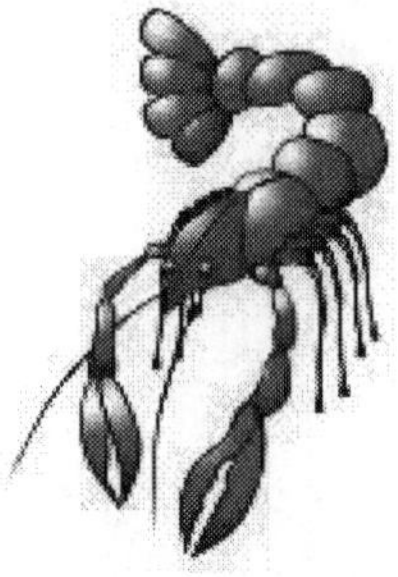

CHAPTER THIRTEEN:
Huntin' An' Trappin; Shrimpin' An' Crabbin'

Dawgs

Me an' Dupree and his olda brudder, Rene, is takin' da dawgs to da swamp today. They been bayin' loud recent nights an' it ain' da moon dey tawkin' to. No siree, dem dawgs saying da time come fo' some huntin' Dem dawgs ready to run. Dey tellin' us to grab up our shotguns an' be ready to hunt us some raccoon.

Rene's gonna cook up a coupla stockpots o' coon stew fo' da weekend party.

Here's da way he cook it:

Take a buncha fat raccoons home an' skin an' gut da buggers. Make sure to pick out alla da pellets. Den berl 'em inna pot for a bit, bones an' all. When dem coons cooked up pull 'em from da pot and cut da meat up in chunks.

Sauté da trinity (onion, celery, green peppa) an' mix dem veg wit da brown roux an' some o' dat coon stock. Spice it all up wit' Tabasco sauce an' black peppa, a liddle salt, an' some chop herbs. Den mix in some chop 'maters an' carrot an an' trow in da coon meat in wit some duck meat. Cook da mess fo' a coupla hours an' serve it all ova rice.

Mmmm, dat good. Dogs always wait fo' a coon meat treat when Rene mak' da stew. Dey know dey earned it, fo' sure.

Coon stew a real treat down her in Bayou country. Much mo' betta dan tree-rat* stew.

Dat's what I say, me.

* squirrel

Da Nutria

Huntin' da raccoons got me tinkin' 'bout da nutria. Big rat like critters is what dem nutria is. Cajun folk been trappin' an' eatin 'em since da nineteen thirties when dey was imported from Sout' America.

Farmers back then thought dey could raise da Nutria for da fur trade, but dat din't work out. Den in a hurricane bust up a Nutria farm an' dem critters escaped into da Bayous. Now dere's millions o' da buggers. Swamp vegetation, rice and sugarcane fields, Bayou dams, and even sewers is bein' messed up by dem Nutria. Got so bad an' da State put up a bounty program fo' da trappers.

Da Cajun dishes dat use Nutria meat is mostly stews, étouffées, an' sometimes da jambalya. Some folk make Nutria sausage.

Outside o' Cajun country mos' folks tink Nutria juss big rats an' dey doan wan't to eat 'em. Doan matta what da outside folks tink. Some o' da fine restaurants in Louisiana is servin' Nutria. Dey call it *Ragondin* an' dat sure sounds fancy. Even though folks doan know 'zactly what dat *Ragondin* is dey eatin' it an' enjoyin' it.

I tink it was ol' Barnum said you can fool some o' da people alla da time.

Da Second Amendment

Down her in Acadiana we're all brought up to be self sufficient. Dat means takin' care o' ourselves and dat furtha means bein' able to live off da land and da wata. We're all born into da huntin' an' da fishin' way o' life.

Long 'bout a Cajun boy's eighth birthday he get his first rifle, usually a Mossberg single shot, a bolt action .22 dat you gotta cock before firin'. A year or so later da .410 shotgun. Growin' up da boys save dey money for better equipment, like da .30-.30 Winchester or da Browning 12 gauge pump. Sometimes da handgun fo' shootin' snakes in da swamplands or da human snakes dat could-might invade da home. Different folks like different gun makers and different kinds o' guns, but dey all want firs' class firearms.

Lately we been hearing a lot o' controversy ova da second amendment to da Constitution o' da United States of America dat deal wit' da right to bear arms. Now, I ain' a lawyer or one o' dem Constitution experts but I do believe dat Americans have da right to own and to use guns fo' good purpose. Problem is da founding fathas weren't tinkin' 'bout nutcases an' criminals in da big cities dey were tinkin' 'bout citizen militias.

I tink da politicians an' da National Rifle Association ought to stop bickerin' an' stand up fo' what's right an' good. Dere's folks dat want to make gun ownin' against da law, an' dat ain't right. Dere's folks dat tink having a gun means dere can't be no regulation. Den dere's other folk who just want some common sense regulation like background checks fo' everybody. Dat make sense an' could-might save some lives.

What I don't believe is dat any nutcase should be allowed to shoot up anything or anybody he want. Ownin' guns is important but so is bein' responsible. Young-uns in the Bayou country is always taught responsibility from da git-go. Dang shame da same ain' true everywhere.

Shrimpin' am Crabbin' Wit' Da Lafitte Skiff

TT Fontenot an' mos' other Shrimpers an' crabbers in da Bayou country fava da Lafitte Skiff fo' dere workboat of choice.

Da Lafitte skiff –15 to 50 feet—wit a shallow draft is designed to work da near shore Gulf watas an' also da inshore creeks and bayou flats. Da traditional skiff is made of wood but modern ones is sometimes fiberglass. Dey are sleek craft with low freeboard an' a wide beam. Da design help wit' da loading an' carrying big payloads of shrimp or crabs. Da skiffs got big inboard motors. Cajun boys like da Chevvy V8s, fixed up fo' marine use.

Makin' da Lafitte style skiff wit a semi-deep vee front an' a flat bottom rear is hard to do so they generally is built in small shipyards by pros. But sometimes da individual fishermen build 'em.

Dere ain' a Cajun boy dat doan want a Lafitte skiff. No siree, not a one.

Da Big Guy

We run inta da big guy from ova to *Breaux Bridge* in da lumber yard dis mornin'. He saw me an' got all bristly. I thought we was gonna have a nudder knock down-slug it out. But, dat din't happen.

Dupree was wit me an' turns out he an da big guy was an ol' army buddies. Dupree smoothed tings ova. Din't hurt none dat Dupree lie some an' tole da big guy dat I was a black belt karate expert an' no one ta fool wit'.

Dupree, he get us ta bury da hatchet an' shake hands, what is okay by me.

Dat Dupree, he's sumptin'. He gotta be da bes' fibber I eva come across.

Anyhoo, Dupree invited da big guy for coon stew an' col' ones on Friday nite. Da big guy says he gonna be dere an' he's bringin' da red head librarian.

Dere ain' gonna be no trouble come Friday, no. I ain' foolin' wit dat redhead.

Gettin' Anxious

Friday come an' Rene got alla da cookers out an' he's makin' da coon stew fo' tonite. Maybe I go down to Dupree's an' hep' him out. I figger he juss might need somebody to sample da stuff, mak' sure it cook up right.

Den again', dat Rene is da crankiest ol' bugga on da Bayou. Could-might be betta ta leave him be an' wait till dis evenin' to taste some o' dat stew.

Best if I stay right here on da porch and watch da 'gators in da Bayou. Maybe read a good book dis afternoon. Pop da top on a col' one or two.

Dat coon stew will wait. An' da longer da stew simma da betta it gonna be. Dat's what I say, me.

Hey, hey-hey, --Ah, ha-ha

I tink you all know by now dat Cajun folk are a hard workin' lot, but when work is done it's done. Dats da time we save fo' play. Drinkin' some col' ones. Dancin' wit' da pretty gals. Havin' a time.

Hey, hey- hey, --Ah, ha-ha. Gettin' into da music --clappin' hands, stompin' feet, shoutin' to da beat.

Havin' our-selves a fine ol' time. Doin' what feels good, what brings da smiles. Having da best o' times, shoutin', *laissez le bon temps rouler*. Cajun men an' da ladies dancin' to da guitars, da fiddles, an' da squeezebox.

Dat's da special Cajun way. Dere ain' nothing better. An' dat's a plain true fact.

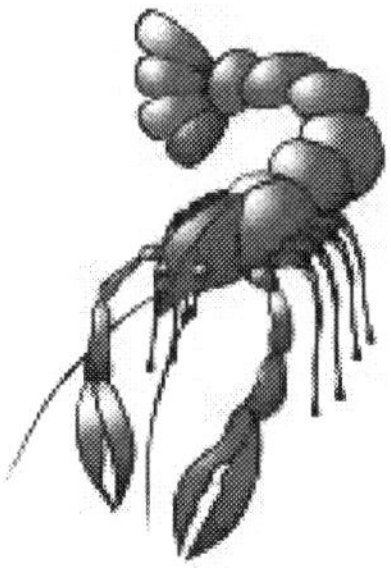

CHAPTER FOURTEEN:
Da Readhead Again

Friday Nite Party

Da Friday nite party down to Dupree's went good fo' da mos' part. Lotsa col' ones settin' on ice. Rene had a buncha cooker full wit dat scrumptious coon stew. Dere was boil shrimp an' crawfish. Lotsa boudin roasted wit' whole okra pods. Da ladies brung dirty rice an tater salad an cole slaw an' stuff. Dupree even made sure da hounds got some o' dat coon stew an' some fresh, warm hush puppies.

Woulda been a perfec' nite 'cept for da mistake by me. I brung my book wit me, a paperback copy o' How The Irish Saved Civilization. Dat's an' interestin' story 'bout dem monks in Ireland' copyin' all da great works o' lit-rat-chur.

TT saw dat book stickin' out of my back pocket an' started raggin' 'bout me knowin' da redhead librarian was comin' an' how I was tryin' to 'press her. Pretty soon da whole gang chimed in. Dey worked me ova good.

Den da big guy an' da redhead gal show up. Afta a while da redhead take to dancin' to da music from Clifton Chenier's *Zydeco* band. She shakin' her booty good an' da town womenfolk get dey backs up. Dey was usin' words like tramp an' hussy. Finally da redhead got tee off an' tole da big guy she want to leave.

Da big guy, who by now was buddyin' up wit all o' da Pigeonaire folk, just laugh an' tole da redhead to cool her jets. Den he say to Dupree dat he gonna dump dat gal.

Afta a bit I see da redhead down by da Bayou, sulkin'. I talk to her for a bit an' finally she perk up some. So, bein' da gentleman dat my momma brung me up to be I give her a ride in my pickup back to her home in *Plaquemines*. Was late when we got dere an' she invite me in to her 'partment.

Da raggin' I'm gonna get when I get back to Pigeonaire in da mornin' gonna be somthin' awful. But dat won't botha me none.

No siree, ain' gonna botha me.

Dat Redhead

If you're wonnerin' now 'bout dat foxy redhead from *Plaquemines*, turns out her name is Colleen Thibodaux. We talk an' talk las' nite an' get to know each odder some. Colleen tole me her *granpere* an' her *granmere* O'Donnell was from a shotgun shack in da Irish Channel in N'Awlins where dey raise a buncha kids. Da oldest o' dere offspring, Colleen's Maman, Bridget, hooked up wit' a Cajun boy, Hugo Thibodaux, a shrimper who sold his catch at da city wharf. Bridget an' Hugo married an' da beauteous Irish-Cajun Colleen came o' dat union.

Dat Colleen, she got a smile melt a' iceberg an' da prettiest freckles to go wit dat smile. An' it turn out that she's real nice, not snooty like I thought.

Dat's da sweetie I took home las' nite. Now, it looks like I juss might be goin' to *Plaquemines* a lot dis year.

But, tonite is da football.

Dem Saints

Good football game on da TV las' nite. Da Sain' beat dem Philadelphia Iggles. How bout dem boys. Dey 'bout as tough as dere is in da NFL. Huh?

Wo-wee, dey is some playas.

Nex' is da NFC championship an' den da supabowl. Dem Sain's could-might go all da way an' den dey get to go to Disney-worl'.

Dey ain' da ol' Sain's o' yester-year no mo', no. Dis bunch is "marchin' in". Dat is, o' course, provided dey doan slip up.

Plaquemines

Goin' run da pick-em-up on ova to *Plaquemines* dis evenin' 'cause dat sweet gal Colleen 'vite me to suppa. She cookin' up a roas' chicken wit stuffin', gravy, mash taters, an' green bean. Dat sure soun' good to me. *Yum.*

We gonna kick back afta dinna an' talk 'bout books an' such. Whateva else we talk 'bout I ain' sayin'. Dat's 'cause what we might be sayin' ain' none o' nobody else's bidness.

An' dat's what I tink, me.

Cajun Tawk

It ain' proper English. It ain' 'zactly French neither. It ain' like anyting you evea heard in all your born days. Dat Bayou language ain' widout a certain lilt. It ain' widout its own unique ways a puttin' stuff. It ain' a skinny way o' talkin, it's more like it's fat wit' alla it's special ways o' gettin' ideas 'cross.

Da Bayou Cajun is da way o' tawkin' throughout sout' Louisiana. I tink it's a pretty good way to say tings. It's special like. Ain' no odder tawk as good as dat Cajun.

Now, I'm finding that when I'm with Colleen I'm not speaking like a Cajun. Words are coming out of my mouth that make me sound like a TV announcer or a schoolteacher or a librarian. I'm using big words like prevaricate an' harbinger when plain simple words like 'lie' and 'like what's coming' will do. That's a problem. I might be losing who I am.

Can't let dat happen, no. Dat's what I tink, me.

Bein' Me

I'm sittin' here on da gallery dis mornin' sippin' on a cup o' coffee/chicory blend an' watchin' da worl' go by. Ol' man Broussard floated by in his john boat a while 'go. Said he was plannin' on bringin' home a string o' *sac-a-lait* fo' lunch. Dem's good eatin' fish. Den Rene an' Dupree stop by to see if I wanna go duck huntin' wit dem. I passed 'cause I gotta start to repair some sidin' an' stuff on Fadda LeBlanc's rectory dis afta-noon.

While sippin on my mornin' java I been tinkin' bout me an' Colleen. She's mos' as Cajun as me an' I tink I been trying to impress her by tawkin' like what ain' natural to me. Nex' time we get together I'm gonna tawk like I allas has. Ain' gonna put on no airs. Juss be me.

I'm bettin' it ain' gonna make no difference to dat gal, no.

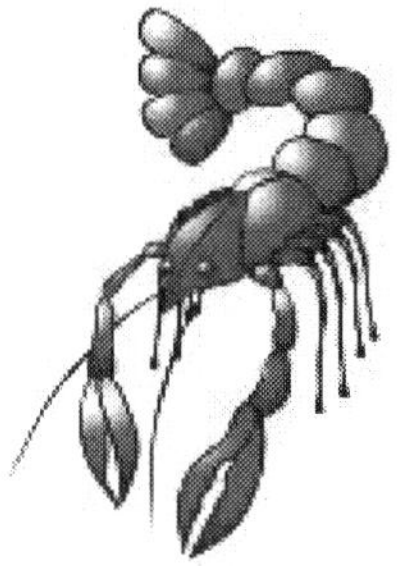

CHAPTER FIFTEEN:
Figgerin' Tings Out

Tawkin' Wit Da Priest

Here it's late fall, nearin' winta an' I worked up a sweat tearin' dat cypress siding offa da east side o' Fadda LeBlanc's rectory. Dem boards got all dry rot an' cracked from to much sun ova da years. Man, dem board was nail on tight wit' dem ring-shank maze nails. Hadda yank real hard on da Wonder bar to loosen 'em up.

Fadda LeBlanc brought out a coupla col' ones to da *gallarie* an tole me to quit fo' da day. Dere's tomorrow he tole me. Time 'nuff to put da new boards on.

We sittin' an sippin' on dose longnecks an' I brung up my concern 'bout Colleen and 'bout me bein' me when I'm near dat beauty.

Da good Fadda laugh an' laugh. Turns out dat Colleen is his niece an' he baptize her when he was da curate at *Sain' Joan D'Arc* in *Plaquemines*.

Da Fadda tell me dere ain' a high falutin' bone in dat gals body an' I ain' got no worries 'bout me bein' me 'round her.

Looks like sittin' and sippin' on a col' one wit da priest is a good ting.

Yessiree, a good ting.

All A-Muddle

Despite da fac' dat Fadda LeBlanc say not to worry 'bout me bein' me I can't help it. Colleen ain' give me reason to believe I shouldn't act like me 'round her.

I tawk to myself 'bout bein' 'zactly who I am. An' it all come down to nuttin'. I'm still nervous 'bout bein' wit' dat gal. Doan know why, but I am.

Hardly got a wink o' sleep last night wit' worryin' 'bout where tings gonna go or not go wit' dat gal an' me. I'm gonna have to think 'bout whether I should continue ta call on Colleen or not. Make my mind up one way or da other.

It ain' no fun dis muddle, no.

Dodgin' Da Bullet

Got a call on my cell phone from dat redhead beauty Colleen. She was all 'cited when she tole me dat she got her a job in New Yawk city wit a big publishin' house. Gonna be a junior editor she say. But she says she's sad dat she's leavin' me behin' when we ain' hardly got to know each odder yet.

Dat's okay, I said. Tol' her sometimes a person gotta do what's bes' fo' herself.

Colleen got a midnight flight from N'Awlins to da Big Apple. I'm gonna take her to *Galitoire*'s in da French Quarta fo' a fine dinna to celebrate her new job. Den I'm gonna take her to da airport.

Look's like I'm gonna dodge a bullet, me.

But still, I'm kinda gonna miss dat sweet gal. Maybe someday I can go on up to da Apple an visit her.

Category Five

Talkin' 'bout da **H**urricane here an' y'all might-could notice I'm usin' da capital "**H**" an' da bold print. Why is dat you ask?

Da answer is 'caust I ain' talkin' 'bout da hurricane dat swirl in from da gulf. No, it's da **H**urricane you get at Pat O'Brien's in N'Awlins. Wit' four ounces of rum and da fruit flava mix poured ova shaved ice da O'Brien **H**urricane pack a category five wallop.

Some folk tink Pat's **H**urricane in da special 26 ounce glass dat's shape like a curvy woman is only fo' da tourist. Dat ain' right, 'cause on da occasions me an' my buddies an' da Cajun gals get to da Crescent city we like to go to Pat's an' get one o' dem **H**urricane. We got lots o' dem tall **H**urricane glasses on da backbar at Dupree's place. Folks bring dem home to *Pigeonaire* an' drop 'em off at our fav-o-rite waterin' hole.

Took Colleen to Pat's after our dinna at *Galitoire*'s. Now dere's two mo' o' dem special glasses to drop of at Dupree's.

Who Do Dat Voodoo Dat You

I'm a Louisiana style Catlic. Dat's to say we got our own ways o' beliving. So one o' my heroine is Marie LeVeau, a Catlic who was also da Queen o' da Voodoo.

Afta havin dem **H**urricanes at Pat's, Colleen an me took the time to visit the priestess's grave, at St. Louis number one, and pay homage. We drew da three crosses (+++) on da side o' Marie's tomb so's we could get a wish if we need it. Used number two pencil dat will wash off next rain an' not deface da marble none.

Marie LeVeau's sprit will know who made dose marks. An' dat's important. One never knows when one is gonna need a liddle Voodoo ju ju.

Dat's what I say, me.

Sadder Dan I Thought

I was kinda confuse. One part o' me says I was dodging da bullet an odder part o' me was sayin' I was gonna miss dat sweet gal.

I only juss met Colleen a short bit of time ago but we had us some good times. Kissin' dat sweet readhead goodbye at da airport was hard. It was sad. Sadder than I thought it was gonna be.

Afraid I'm gonna miss bein' wit dat sweetie. An' dat's da troof.

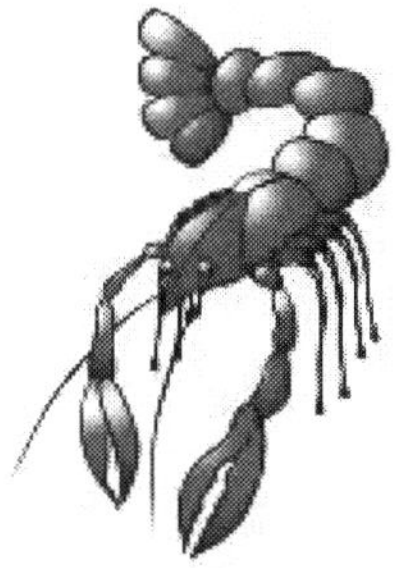

CHAPTER SIXTEEN:
Two Wheelin' It

Motacycle

Da kickin' back, like all good tings, need to come to an end. It's time now to get back to da work . Gotta make me some money. Got my eye on a fine ol' Harley dat Herve Broussard just finish restorin'. Dat's one nice bike, flame paint job, lotsa chrome, big ol' buddy seat, leatha saddle bags. Da whole nine yards.

Dupree say dat I'm losin' my mind if I buy dat bike. He says I'll bust my bones.

Dat could-might be a fact, but I cain' let da facts tell me how to live life. Still, I could-might think it ova before buyin' da machine.

But, maybe not.

I'll tink 'bout 'zactly what to do later. Right now, evening comin' on.

Sun In Da Western Sky

One o' da truly wonderfil tings 'bout livin' in da Bayou country is da sundowns. Dey are spectacular. Especially beautiful are da western skies in da winta. Da sun is low an' at dat time in da evenin' da sky lights up wit' pinks an' reds on a blue backgroun' dat slowly fades to grey an' den to da dark o' nite. Dat's one beautiful show an' dere ain' two nites dat it's da same.

Not only does da sky light up at sundown, da bayou watas do too. Da fading rays o' da sun send shimmers of gold an silver an' platinum across da ripplin' surface an' paint an amazin' picture. Sometimes dere's deep purple hues.

It's a privlege an' a pleasure seing dem nightly light shows coverin da sky and da bayou wata.

Dat's what I tink, me.

Come Mornin'

Come morning one has to look da odder way. Da mornin' sky even if it ain' never as spectacular as da evenin' sky is a welcome sight. Dat sky have its own beauty wit' da sun peekin' up from da east.

Warmin' sun rays of mornin' go good wit' a hot cuppa chicory coffee. Me, I like sittin on da gallery an' sippin' da coffee before going off to work da day. It's a nice quiet time before getting on da job an' hearin' da rat-tat-tat o' da nail guns and da screechin' o' da skill saws.

Yessir, early mornin' time is a fine time.

Monday

Monday come again an' I gotta get to work. Dem Sain' been losin' lately an' causin' da flattenin' out o' my wallet. Dat's a sad state dat has gotta be corrected. So, it's off to da lumba yard to get dat special old-timey cypress sidin' to finish off da job on Fadda LeBlanc's rectory.

Get da rectory job done an' get paid. Then I juss might have 'nuff cash fo' a down payment on da Harley.

Da bike got a 88 cubic inch Shovelhead long block all chrome up nice. Den dere's da flame paint job an' da tall ape hangas. Got da skinny fron' tire an' da fat back un. Chrome spoke wheels. Dat's some nice bike.

Betta get to work now. Get dat money, me.

Da *Acadian Boucherie*

Da fall o' da year is comin' an' tradition in the Bayou country is to have da community hog butchering party, da *Acadian Boucherie*, when summa is done. Cajuns use every part o' da pig in dere cookin' recipes except da squeal. If dey could figga out what to do wit' da squeal dey'd use that too. Autumn is da time afta da heat o' summa an' before da col' of winta dat's best for preparin' da hog.

Modern times is such dat da *Acadian Boucherie* is becomin' almos' a ting o' da past. Mos' younger Cajuns get dere meat from da supermarket or da specialty meat shop. Still dere's an occasional *Boucherie* to be found in *Acadia*.

Dupree's olda brudder Rene head up an annual hog *fête* in our liddle town of Pigeonaire. Dere's butcherin' da cuts o' da pork, an' dere's sausage makin', an dere's da cookin' o da cracklin's. Dere's stuff cookin' all da day.

Wimmenfolk bring da side dishes an' da desserts. O' course dere's plenny o' col' ones in da ice tubs.

Rene, he make da best lip-smackin' *Boudin* an' also lip smackin' cracklin's. Wit' Rene's delicious offerin's at da *Acadian Boucherie* we always have da best of times.

Cajun Tanksgivin'

Wit' da Autumn dere's Tanksgivin's comin' before to long. Fo' dat holiday we gonna have us a feast, yes siree.

About two days before da Tanksgivin' dinner I go out to the coop, me. Select a big ole fat turkey, an' a plump duck, an' a roastin' chicken. Chop they head off. Den I debone dem buggers, 'ceptin' for they wings, an' dey legs, an' dey thighs.

I take an' shove da duck inna turkey and da chicken in da duck.

Now, dat main feast o' poultry ain' quite ready for da oven yet. Gotta stuff him some mo'.

Fo' da stuffin' I tink I'll use dirty rice and *boudin* wit some chop mudbug tail meat. Cousin Arnol' got him a Lafittte skiff and he kin get me some oyster. Shove dat fat mollusk meat up the part of da chicken dat go over da fence last and nestle it deep in da rice and sausage stuffin'.

Now we got what da Cajun folk call da 'turducken'. Take a lot a slicin' trough alla dat meat and stuffin'' to finally get to da special treat. Ow-whee though, I'm gonna enjoy dat succulent oyster, me. Wash him down wit a glass a good wine.

Me, I'll even share some wit' good friends.

Houn' Dog Beer

Was settin' on da gallery earlier dis mornin' readin from da *Times Picayune* an' I run 'cross dis liddle article 'bout a lady in da Netherlands, ova dere in Holland somewhere, brewing' beer fo' her houn' dogs. Seem she think after a day in da woods if she enjoy a col' one or two so should' her huntin' hounds. Da lady brews beer fo' dem dogs from beef broth' an' malt.

Dat's damn foolish. Hounds doan need no beer. Dey plenny satisfied getting' to lap up a share o' da cookin' done from wha' gets shot in da woods. Dat's what I tink, me.

But, 'nuff said 'bout houn' dog beer. I gotta get finish up on da Fadda's rectory today.

Ain' Gonna Happen

Herve say he ain' gonna let me test drive his mota-cycle. He says he rememba da las' time I tried out a fo' sale bike. Bugga kicked out when I twisted da throttle. Me an' dat motacycle got us messed up some.

Herve sayin' he doan care so much 'bout me gettin' bust up but dere's no way in heaven he gonna let dat happen wit his restored mota-bike. If dat Boy ain' gonna let me try out da machine den dere ain' no way he gonna sell it to me. I neva buy no pig in da poke. An' dat's da troof.

Beggin' Herve

Da job on Fadda LeBlanc's rectory is done an' da place look as good as da day it was built in 1801. Da bronze historic register plaque is even nail back on da galleria wall. Da priest pay me an' I went to see Herve's choppa motacycle. Dat motacycle was all shine up an' sure did look good.

Me, I hadda beg an' plead, but finally Herve cave in an' handed me da keys. I cranked da bike up fo' da test drive. Revved da throttle good, kicked da bike into gear, an' popped da clutch.Dat bike buck up an' dump me on my *patoot*. Hurt sumptin' awful. Den to make mattas worse da bike skittered off da road an into da Bayou. Herve say dat bike went down unda da wata like one o' dem ball o' lead dey use on da Sportfisha deep sea downrigger in da Gulf. Dey had a hard time hookin' da winch cable to dat bike to haul it out.

Now, here I am in da horsepistol afta havin' my tail bone put back in place. Dere's a lump size of a sofball on da back o' my head an' it's real tenda. An' I gotta spen' more money dan I have to pay fo' da Sawbones puttin' my coccyx back were it belong, not to mention payin' Herve fo' a motacycle what might neva run no mo'.

Da Redhead Comin' Home

Da only good ting is Fadda LeBlanc come an' visit me. He says his red head niece's job in da Apple din't work out. Sumptin' 'bout dem big city folk bein' too rough an pushy fo' her taste. Colleen comin' back home to da Cajun country where she belong.

Now, I'm gonna need to get me some money to court dat sweet gal. Where will da money come from? Dat's what I need to figger out, me.

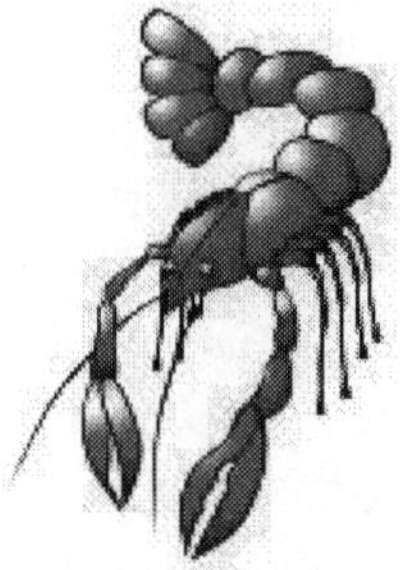

CHAPTER SEVENTEEN: Goin' In To Bidness?

Now I Gone An' Done It Again

I got let outta da horsepistol yesteddy. My back end is still a liddle sore but I'm getting' 'round okay. Now I juss might a done gone an' cause me anotha problem.

Fadda LeBlanc been braggin' on da good job he tink I done on da rectory. Da word goin' roun' da Cajun country dat I know wha' in da debbil I'm doin'.

A rich guy from N'Awlins hear I'm good at workin' on da old buildings like da plantation houses dat line da River road. Some frien' o' da priest put in da good word.

Da rich guy contact me. Seems he bought da ol' *Sain' Helene* plantation up to West *Feliciana* Parish an' he need someone to restore da antebellum main house an a bunch o' dependencies too.

I tol' him sure I can do da work an' dat did da trick. Man say he'll have a contrac' ready fo' me to sign by Monday. *Whoee*, I can sure stick my foot in it sometime.

Now I gotta get a crew o' fellers dat know what dey doin' An' I'm prayin' da banker, ol' grump, Pierre LeMatin, gonna len' me da money fo' da special tools we gonna need to duplicate antebellum woodwork an' such. Den I'm gonna have ta boss dem guys and make sure o' da payroll an' da witholdin' an' all dat odder bidness stuff.

Might-could be dat Colleen can handle da office stuff fo' me. Dat gal gonna need a job when she get back here from da Apple.

Could- might also be I need to go to Fadda LeBlanc's church an' do some prayin'. Got me a chance ta get on da road to bein' rich, me. But I'm gonna need all o' da help I can get to pull dis bidness stuff off. Fingers crossed.

Cookin' *écrevisse*

Later I got to figger out 'bout how to do da bidness stuff, but now it's da weekend comin' on. We gonna do a mudbug boil down to Dupree's roadhouse. We cookin' up 'bout five-six pots o' lip smackin' *écrevisse* (dat's crawfish or mudbugs for those of y'all what doan know). Key is dat da cookin' o' dem *écrevisse* doan work at all unless you got a bunch o' col' beer.

Here's da way to do da *écrevisse*:

Put da basket in da 20 gallon cookpot half full o' water and add six ounce o' da cookin' oil (da oil make gettin' da meat outta da crawfish shell easy.) Add one small bottle o' liquid crab boil (Zatarain's is good). Drink a col' one. Add 10-12 bay leaves, a cup o' Tabasco sauce, tree pounda o' onion. Drink a nudder col' one. Squeeze two dozen lemon and pour in da juice. Drop da lemon hafs in too.

Now five pound o' whole redskin taters. Cook fo' fifteen minutes.

Now's a good time for a col' one. You can rinse da crawfish while you drinkin' da beer. Best way is put da whole 40 pound bag in a wire basket an' hose dem buggas down. When da mud is gone dump them crawdads in a cooler wit' da drain open an' rinse again, den put 'em to da side.

You gonna need anudder beer while you husk a dozen ear o' corn an' cook 'em. 10-15 minutes. Pull da basket wit' da corn an' onion an' taters an' put 'em in a big container fo' later.

Now you gonna cook da crawfish. Put the basket back in da pot.

- One sack o' crawfish boil.

- Da whole container of Tone's Cayenne Pepper (yup, da entire container)
- Stir da stuff for about a minute.
- Add da *écrevisse*. Bring up to a roiling Boil.

Cook fo' 'bout five minute, turn da heat off, an' soak fo 10-15 minutes. Dump onto da picnic table covered wit butcha papa and eat 'em wit da potatos, onion, an' corn.

Gotta have a col' one wit dem *écrevisse*.

Da forty poun' bag makes 'bout 10 pound o' crawfish meat or 'nuff fo a couple o' Cajun guys.

We cook a lot o' *écrevisse*. Keep five-six pot a boilin' at one time. Eatin' dem succulent morsels is *les bon temps*.

Suck Da Heads

At da *écrevisse* boil most o' da meat is in da mudbug tail, but you can get youself a liddle from da claws. Dat sweet white meat from da mudbugs is some scrumptious good eatin'. A Cajun boy can eat a belly full of dat meat.

Fo' da real treat, one dat's heaven on da eart', suck da crawfish heads. *Mmmmmm*! Wondaful! Dat's what I tink, me.

Try doin' it and dat will be what you tink, too.

Da State O' Da State O' Louisiana

Dere was a story in da Times-Picayune dis mornin' 'bout what States is da unhealthiest. Louisiana da winna again, seem we da mos' unhealthy State.

Dat stuff 'bout Louisiana bein' bad fo' folk's health got me to tinkin'. Wonderin' if it's alla dem chemical plants an' refineries on da River road dat's causin' da problem.

Dey call dat strip from *Chalmette* on up past *Baton Rouge* cancer alley. If it's cancer alley what is da root o' da problem den I'm a bit relieved. We can clean up dat mess if we got da will.

But, it could-might be da Cajun cookin' dat's puttin' Louisiana up to number one in unhealthy.

Might-could find out it's dat brown roux, an' andouille sausage, an pulled pig, an' all o' our other Bayou country vittles is what's unhealthy.

Dat wouldn't be good, no. Could be a disasta. I'm worried, me.

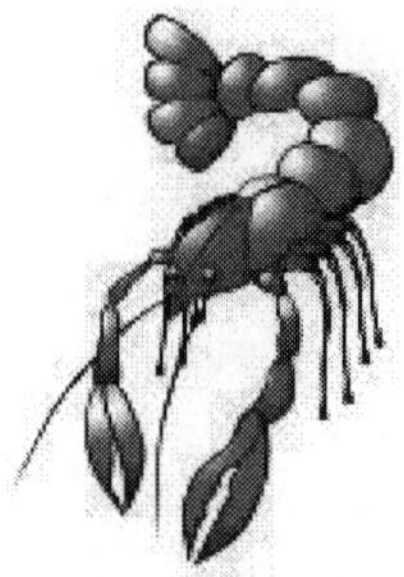

CHAPTER EIGHTEEN:
Gettin' Da Bidness Up an' Runnin'

Getting' Da Woodworka Aboard

Gonna pick up Colleen at da N'Awlins airport dis evenin'. Sure be good seein' dat redhead gal again. Las' night we tawk an' she agreed to do da office work fo' my new venture.

Dat gal's full ideas. She say her cousin, Mikey "Knuckles" LeDieux is a fine woodworka. Says he expert at duplicatin' da antebellum trim. Says we should get him on da job.

Dere's a hitch to getting' Knuckles. He's servin three to five in Angola prison fo' aggravated assault. Tings got outta hand at a *Zydeco* festival in Morgan City las' summa an' Knuckles got da blame fo' crackin' some haids. Colleen says Knuckles was railroaded an' we need to get work release fo' him.

I dunno. Workin' tings out wit da State prison board ain' gonna be easy, no.

Pullin' Da String

Dat Colleen is one smart cookie. She got togetha wit' Judge Arnol' LeDieux who is Knuckle's momma's cousin a coupla times remove. Dat make him some kinda shirttail relative to Knuckles an' to Colleen as well.

Colleen played up dat ol' blood bein' ticker dan wata routine an' da judge went fo' it. Word is dat da man has allas been a sucka for a sweet tawkin', good lookin', gal and Colleen is nuttin' if not both o' dem things.

Anyhoo, Judge LeDieux yank hard on da strings. Da judge kinda tink o' hisself as God wit' da powa he got up to Baton Rouge. He not only got Knuckles a work release, he got him a permanent prison furlough.

Da catch is I gotta vouch fo' Knuckles an' make sure he got a place to live an' dat he behave. Oh well, I got dat spare room in da house an' da rent money ain' gonna hurt.

Doan tink nuttin' is gonna go wrong. Leas' wise I'm hopin' not.

Waitin' On Da Bureaucrats

Judge LeDieux did his string pullin' an' got Knuckles da furlough from da State penitentiary. Now we waitin' on dose prison bureaucrats to get da paper work done. Colleen an' me drove on up dere to Angola dis mornin' and dem paper shufflas say dere ain' no problem. Dey juss gotta work out a liddle hitch in da furlough is what dey say.

Da hitch is dat Knuckles have to be back to da prison on da twenty-one and twenty-two o' April. Seems da guy is da bes' bull rider dat eva served time at da prison farm. Sprung from da work farm or not, da Warden ain' 'bout to lose dat talent. Not when da spring rodeo is comin' up on dem dates.

Warden wantin' Knuckles ridin' bulls in da Angola rodeo seem reasonable to me. An' fo' da life o' me I doan know what's so difficul' 'bout da papawork. Bureaucrats can drive a soul plumb bats.

Da Oysta Roast

Gettin' Knuckles outta da work-farm calls fo a celebration am' one o' da good tings we Cajun folk love is da oysta roast. Dat's what we gonna do. Da "R" months (Septemba trough April) is when da oystas are in season. Dey best in da winter months.

Rightly speakin' da oysta ain' roasted at all, dey steamed. Here's how.

Get a coupla bushels o' Gulf oystas and wash 'em down real good wit' da hose. Den make a fire either in a pit or a charcoal or propane cooka. Put a big piece o' quarta inch sheet steel supported by concrete blocks ova da pit fire or right on toppa da grates on da cooka. Dump a buncha oysters on da sheet steel an' cover 'em wit' wet burlap sacks. Dey done when da oystas open up.

We Cajun boys make our own oysta table for crowdin' around. Dem table have a hole in da middle an' a trash can underneath for da shells. An' when you ain' usin' da special oysta knife on dem mollusks you can stab it right into da table top where it's handy to get at for da next oysta.

Dump da oystas onna table. Da oysta table has to have horseradish coctail sauce, Tabasco sauce, saltine crackas, an rolls o' paper towels.

Da oystas goes best wit' a Cajun boil, dat's shrimps, taters, corn on da cob, onion, an' andouille sausage. Some folks also have da chili dogs at da oysta roast. An' o' course, *beaucoup* longnecks.

Oysta roast is a lip smackin' good treat. But, remember, doan eat dem oystas dat refuse to open, dey ain' no good, could-might make a body sick.

Tings Was Goin'

Tings was goin' good til tings went bad. Me an' Colleen went on up to Angola an' pick up her cousin Knuckles. Brung him on home to Pigeonaire an' got him settle in da spare bedroom at my house on da *Teche*.

We got da restoration job goin' an Knuckles work was outstandin' good. Dat boy's an artis' wit' wood. Not only is Knuckles a real craftsmen, he's a born teacher. He got da whole crew hummin' along like a well oiled machine.

Den da trouble.

Knuckles an' me get on da job at da crack o' dawn. We was pullin' up to da work site an' I see a coupla boys loadin' our lumba to da bed of a pickup. I jump outta da truck an' go to confront them an' one o' dose boys pull out a pistol an' he shoot me.

Knuckles run up an grab da guy an' dang near broke his neck. Den he grabs a hunk o' two by four an' takes afta da odder one. I call 911 on da cell phone an' da Sheriff's boys show up an' arrest dem lumba tiefs. Dey grab Knuckles too.

Turn out okay in da end. My wound was only a scratch where da bullet graze my hip. Da bullet did ruin a good pair o' Duluth Trading Company overalls though.

Knuckles not only got out a jail he was commendated fo' bustin' up *tiefs* what had been stealin' from construction sites fo' more dan a year. By the time Judge LeDieux got through Knuckles had a full pardon from da Governor.

Knuckles still did have to agree to go back to Angola to ride in da big spring rodeo.

Bes' of all I got lotta luvin' attention from Colleen who refuse to accept my wound was just a trifle. An' dat attention ain' no bad ting, no.

Soon as da plantation house restoration is done it will time fo' da celebratin'. We all gonna have a anodder big Cajun style party down to Dupree's place.

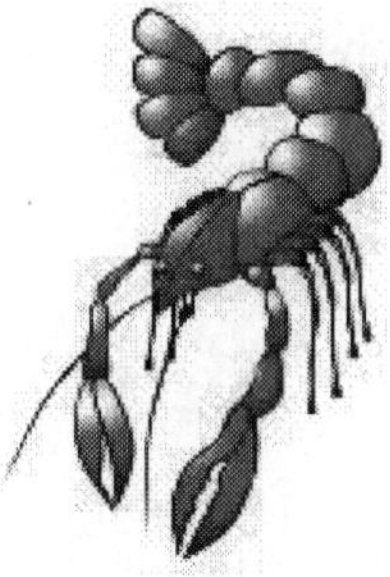

CHAPTER NINETEEN:
Da Cousins At Each Odder

Drivin' Colleen Bats

Colleen's cousin, Knuckles, has been a problem since da downturn in da economy trow a monkey wrench in our reconstruction bidness. Dat boy is a wood workin' wonder but it's turnin' out we ain't got enough contracts to keep us busy as we might like to be. When Knuckles got time on his hands seems he can't help but use it to get himself in one pickle or anudder.

Firs' da boy get arrested for racin' his slick 1967 SS Chevvy Malibu ragtop through town. Chief Antoine Dumon say he got caught doin' better dan a hunnert. Damn fool, he got glass-pacs on dat car's big block 454 an' dey announce him comin' coupla mile away.

Anyhoo, we had to get up five-hunnret plus court costs to get Knuckles outta dat one. Den, he go an' get in a fist-fight ova some hussy what was dancin' in one o' dem nudie bars out on da highway.

Dat fracas ova a nudie dancer embarrass Colleen somethin' awful. She mad as a hornet wit' Knuckles. Chewin' him our every chance she get.

Good ting dere's some distraction here in Pigeonaire dat keep Colleen from dwellin' on Knuckles' behavior. Yesterday she help set up fo' da party we had down to Dupree's place las' night. We had anudder *écrevisse* boil an' dat was some good eatin', 'specially wit' da slaw, an' hush puppies, an' a buncha col' ones.

Me, I'm juss hopin' Knuckles doan get in no mo' trouble an' dat Colleen calm herself down.

Caught In Da Middle

I been runnin' roun' all week tryin' to get tings on an even keel. Firs' Colleen mad at her cousin 'cause he been doin' stupid stuff. Den Knuckles get hard headed an' tell me to tell Colleen to go jump in da Bayou.

Dat's da las' ting I'm goin' to tell dat girl, me.

Hoo-wee, I doan know how I always get in da middle o' contratemps?

Colleen an' Knuckles Cooled Down Some

Took all week but dem two hothead cousins finally calm down an' quit yellin' at each odder. Knuckles is back at work on a new contrac' we manage to latch on to. Colleen is busy wit da company books an' figurin' how to dodge as much tax as she can. Tings has calm down.

It's Friday again an' we all gonna relax tonite. Go down to Dupree's place fo' da fish fry. Kick back. Avoid da contratemps. Dat's what I'm plannin', me.

Fish Fry

Da Broussard boys, K-Paul an' Herve , an' TT promise to get a big batch o' *sac-a-lait* fo' tonight. Rene cookin' up red bean an' rice an' slaw. Da ladies bringin' odder good vittles.

Here's da way to do da fish:

Clean dem *sac-a-lait*. If you ain' from da Bayou da fish also called crappie (dat's pronounced like da farmer's crop).

Shake some salt, an black peppa, an cayenne peppa on da fish. Now coat dem fish wit' some yella mustard.

Put dem fish in a big paper bag wit' fish fry mix (a mix o' fine ground corn meal and flour wit' spices for a old timey flava) an' shake to coat 'em.

Get da peanut oil in da deep fry cooker real hot and fry dem fish till dey golden brown an' crispy. Drain dem fish an serve 'em on tin beer trays.

Dat's some good eatin' at da Friday nite fish fry.

Gonna be some fiddle an 'cordion music, too. An' dancin'. Some o' da older men will prolly get a game o' *bourré* goin' while their ladies gossip.

We gonna have some fun.

Dat *Bourré*

Dere's some real tough joints on the back roads in Bayou country. Cypress shacks built on pilin's wit' bars an' back rooms fo' da gamblin'. I've been in some o' dose places an' I seen plenty, me. Drunk boys bustin' knuckles over the flirty girlies, not ta mention da fights over da cards. An' I seen plenty o' ol' men sittin' an' sippin' their long neck Jax, dem ol' guys long past their fightin' days.

In da back rooms dere's games goin' on mos alla' da time. Mos' common game is *bourré*, da Cajun five card game wit trump cards an' tricks. Sometimes da stakes get way up high and da playas get tempted to cheat some. Dem's da times if you gonna play *bourré* you betta unsnap the haft o' dat thin blade fish scalin' knife on your belt, 'cause, man-o-man, you juss gonna need dat knife, maybe.

I been in dem card games once or twice, but I ain' goin' near those back rooms no mo'. I neva been a fighta; I ain't neva looked for no fightin', no. Hope I neva find myself in a tough joint again but if I do I'm gonna sit at da bar wit da ol' guys and sip my col' one real quiet like.

O' course da *bourré* games at Dupree's place ain' neva cutthroat like in dem tough joints.

Downer

Come home from da job dead tired beat. Me an' Knuckles spent da day demolishin' ol' plaster walls in a River Road mansion. Plaster dust an' horse hair in da air all day. Miserable hot. Talk 'bout sweat o' da brow, dat job was it.

Knuckles drop me off ta home an' dere in da yard is a flame paint Harley motacycle.

Hot damn, I figger Dupree had it all wrong an' dat sweet gal Colleen gone an' bought dat bike fo' me. Whoo-boy, dis guy's one happy fella.

I get me inside da house an' dere on da coffee table is a fancy crash helmet, girly flowers painted on it. Dat strike me as weird.

In da kitchen I ova-hear Colleen on da phone (I figger wit her sista) tellin' all 'bout da motacycle she done bought fo' herself. I turn 'rond, go out da door, an' head fo' Dupree's place.

Coupla col' longnecks might-could smooth out my disappoint-ment, maybe.

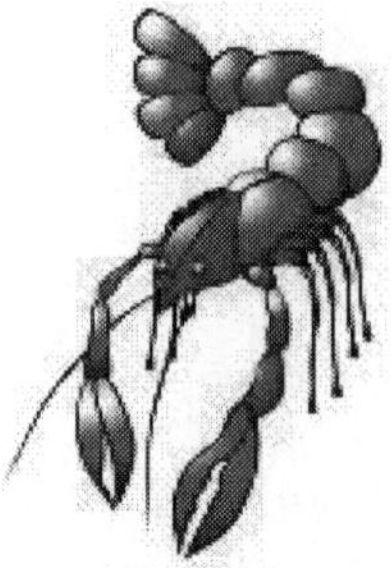

CHAPTER TWENTY:
Times, Dey Ain' So Good

Hard Times

Tings ain' goin' so good down here on da Bayou dis year.

We got us a liddle bit o' work, but da antebellum plantation house restoration bidness all but dry up. Dem Hurricane dat make a mess o' sou' wes' Louisianna an Texas a while back scare da banks an' insurance companies. Dey ain' lending money an' dey ain' writin' policies. An' dat sure slow da bidness.

Den dere's been da oil spill in da Gulf makin' mattas worse.

Knuckles skirtin' da law again an' we had to bail him twice. An' addin' to da misery Fadda LeBlanc getting' restless 'bout me an' Colleen an what he call our state o' bein'. He doan come right out an say dat livin' together without da sacrament o' matrimony is a big ol' mortal sin but dat's what he imply wit' comments he been makin'.

Neither one o' o' us is enjoyin' da pressure comin' from Fadda LeBlanc not to mention from our odder relatives an friends. We both happy wit' tings just as dey be and doan need no 'vice from nobody, but we been gettin' it just da same.

I'm hopin', an' I know Colleen is hopin' too, dat nex' year gonna be a better dan dis year.

Time'll tell. Dat's what I say, me.

Da Swamp

Dey's trouble in da swamp ever since dem hurricane, Katrina an' Rita, come tru here an' it's worser now afta da big oil spill in da gulf. Bad trouble.

Usta be folks could mak' good money hirin' out blinds to Yankee duck hunters. Now, dem Yankees say da swamp look like da grass been kilt by a hard frost. We ain' ever had dat frost down here in Cajun country, but dat swamp grass sure 'nough dead.

Ain' no ducks. Ain' no hunters. Ain' no dollas.

Havin' a bad time, us.

MR. GO

Sum-bitch, dat **Mr. Go**, make da hurricanes worse than dey should be. **MR-GO**, odderwise known as da Mississippi River Gulf Outlet, was dredged by da Army Corps of Engineers in da 1960s. He's a cut seventy-six mile thru da cypress swamp an' he's been slow killing' off our Cajun way. Dem engineer make da shortcut for big freighter an' tanker goin' to and fro the Gulf of Mexico and dat ole Mississippi river.

Politicians figger **Mr. Go** seem like a good idea at the time. But da saltwater been leachin' da levees for 'bout half a century now an' slow but sure killin' off da marshes.

Now Katrina an' dem other storms come and bust up **Mr. Go**. Da levees all 'bout washed away. Docks is gone. Houses are smash to sticks.

Dem politican an' Corps of Engineer suppose ta help da folk, but I doan know. Dat **Mr. Go** 'bout finish our Cajun way an' ain' nobody up in Baton Rouge or Washington dat give a hoot.

Breach o' Trust

Dere a chasm `tween Bayou folk an' da bigshots. Dat breach run deep as da Gulf waters where da Horizon rig done blow up. Da Gulf o' Mexico is where much of our livelihood is, wit' da shrimp, da fish, an' yeah, even wit' dat black gold.

Da gubmint doan know what to do; da oil company ain't helpin' much; da Bayou folk just takin' it on da chin.

Da marsh, she dyin'. Da pelican, da egret, da 'gator dey all slick wit' oil. *Beaucoup* glob o' dat goo coat da green salt grasses an' turn `em all ugly dead.

Flyovers by corporate big shots ain' da answer. Da President yellin' 'he gonna do some ass kickin' ain' nuttin' but blusta.

Dey all tawk an' tawk `bout top kills, `bout junk shots, `bout concrete boxes, an' all manner of stuff to kill da leak. It's plain an' simple none o' dat stuff works. Da black gold keep on spewin'.

Finally, dey got a cap put on da well da oil gushin' from an' it seem to be working. Now, dey need to get dem relief wells drilled an' cemented in. Den dey can give us da wherewithal dat we need fo' da cleanup.

We ain' engineers, we ain' politicians, an' we ain' bureaucrats; we plain folk. We tradesmen. We caprenters. We fishers an' shrimpers. We oilmen, roughnecks an' roustabouts. We know da waters, da Bayous, da marshes. We know what need doin' an' we know the how o' doin' it.

Da big oil company an' da gubmint can step aside. Da so called experts can step aside. Dey can all juss get outta da way. We'll clean da mess up.

Dat's what I say, me.

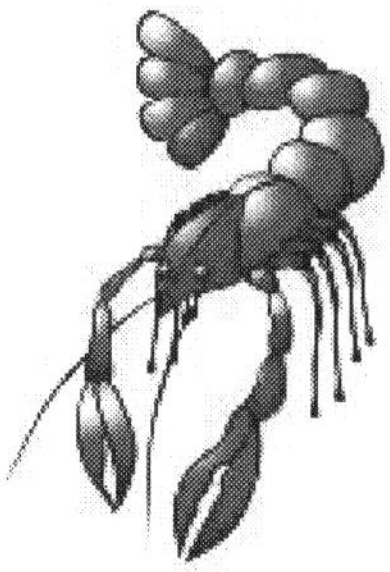

CHAPTER TWENTY ONE:
Winter's Chill Breath

Da Weatha

Da tempratura 'bout freezin' dis mornin' an' dat ain' good, no. Bayou boys like me like da warm weatha an' dat's why we live here in da sout' of Louisiana. Well, dat las' statement ain' entirely da troof. Our ancestors left Nova Scotia cause of a cold political climate, fact is they was chased out. But, ova da generations we come to love da warm Bayou country an' we sure doan like today's cold dang weatha. Makes a body shiver.

Maybe a coupla col' ones down to Dupree's could warm this Cajun fella up.

Da Evangeline Oak

Tinkin' 'bout Nova Scotia an' da ancestors got me to rememberin' 'bout da oak an' da Evangeline legend. Dat old Evangeline oak is in Sain' Martinville on Bayou *Teche*. Da tree is named for the heroine of the poem dat fella Henry Wadsworth Longfellow wrote.

Evangeline was supposed to be a true story 'bout *Acadians* kicked from *Acadie* by da British. Da poem is partly set in sout' Louisiana and names local places such as the *Atchafalaya* an' *Bayou Teche*, and *St. Martin* and *St. Maur*. Da poem tells 'bout da tragedy o' the separation of two lovers Evangeline an' Gabriel.

Some say da troot is dat a gal, *Emmeline Labiche*, and a boy, *Louis Arceneaux*, were da real people what inspired dat Longfellow fella. Legend is dat da British tore *Emmeline* an' *Louis* apart. Later, *Emmeline* got to Maryland an' eventually wound up in Louisiana. Dere under dat ancient oak tree in Sain' Martinville *Emmeline* met wit' *Louis* once again but by dat time he was married. Legend says *Emmeline* lost her mind, withered away an' died.

Dat legend o' da Evangeline oak is one sad story whetha or not it's da whole troof. Lotsa folk, an' dey ain' all from da Bayou country, believe da legend. An' dat a good ting, I think, me.

Freeze A Fella's Patoot

It's still cold in da Bayou country but colder up nort'. It say in da *Times Picayune* dat it's minus forty up in Minneapolis, Minne-sota where da headwaters o' our mighty Mississippi form. Cold as dat Minneapolis is it seems da river source could-might form inta one giant ice cube. Dat happens den alla da wata south o' Minneapolis gonna run downstream an' out to da gulf. Leave da Bayou country high an' dry.

Dat ain't no good, no.

Da odder ting bout da awful cold is a man could freeze his *patoot* off. Dat's bad.

Doan want da cold from up nort', but dem Minnesota folk can ship their cold beer down here. We'll take da suds.

Dat's all what I have to say 'bout dat.

Ain' Warmed Yet

Still col' here in da Bayou country. We ain' used to dis weatha an' we ain' prepared. Leastwise none of us is prepared but Colleen.

Dat gal worked up to New York City fo' a bit an' she purchase winter duds when she was up nort'. Figgered when she come back down here she'd pack them duds away an' neva wear dem no mo'. She figger wrong.

Sadday nite we was all down to Dupree's place an shiverin'. Colleen come in an' she wearin' a Northface down coat, a wool scarf, muckluc booters, an a knit hat pulled down to her eyebrows. She laughin' an' jokin bout our shiverin' an braggin' on her Eskimo outfit.

I figger if I'm eva gonna warm up, I'm gonna have to rub nose wit' Colleen. Then I gonna haul her home an maybe do some odda Eskimo tricks.

Dat's what I tink, me.

Hangin' Da Head

Sunday come an' oh me. *Damnation. Horsefedders. Phooey.* Watchin' da game an' dem Sain' let me down. Can't believe wha' happen. Disgustin'.

Dere was some oil engineer guys from Chicago come on into Dupree's place. Dey was makin' bets. Takin' our money. My wallet been about empty out.

Worse o' all Dupree ran outta col' ones. Dupree an' his brudda, Rene, had to scoot me outta da place 'fore I haul off on dem fancy likker drinkin' Chicago boys.

Maybe las' week comin' back on me. Back then I was laffin' at some Philadelphia Iggles fans dat was in Dupree's at gametime an' dat could-might be da reason fo' the bad luck today.

Whatever da reason, it's a sad day in da great State o' Louisiana; even sadda in N'Awlins. Saddest down to Dupree's roadhouse.

Dem Sain' ain' marchin' in, no.

Stayin' Inside

We in da grip o' dis col' weatha down here to da Bayou country an' I ain' goin' nowhere dis day. Colleen an' me, we gonna stay home an' snuggle under da blanket and watch da TV. Dat's 'zactly what we gonna do.

My cousin, GC, from up in Lowcountry o' Sout' Carolina call las' night an' tell me dey got a rare snow forcast fo' da mornin'. Cold as it is here in sout' Louisiana we ain' getting' none o' dat white stuff.

GC say da snow doan matta none to him. Him an' his hunny-bun gonna keep warm wit' good vittles an' champagne at a neighborhood brunch party dey been invited to.

Dat sounds good to me.

But still, I ain' goin' outside today. Neither is Colleen, no. We're stayin' put til a least Supa Bowl Sunday.

Proselytizin'

We was inside snugglin' from da cold an' a knock come to da door. It was dem preacher folk come down here to da Bayou country from up north Louisiana. Dey peddlin' some new-fangle religion. Sayin' if we 'scribe to da knowledge an' fellaship dey pushin' we gonna, *hallelujah*, see dat white light wha' save our souls.

Now, I'm as curious as da next fella, me. But dat *hallelujah* horsefeathers juss doan ring true. Besides, dey oughta know dey wastin' time down here. Bayou folk is Catlics. Dey alreddy got their religion. Ain' no one gonna lissen to dem bible thumpers.

An', dat's da troof.

Supa Bowl

We down to dat part o' da NFL playoffs where dere only four teams left an' dangit ain' one o' dem N'Awlins. What we got here is da Boston Patriots, da Niners, dem Denver Bronca, an' da Seahawks. *Phooey!* Ain' one o' dem so call football teams dat can stir me up fo' da rootin'. We needed dem Saint to come marchin' in, but dey din't.

Still, alla dis won't keep me from downin' a coupla col' ones down to Dupree's place on Supa Bowl Sunday, no.

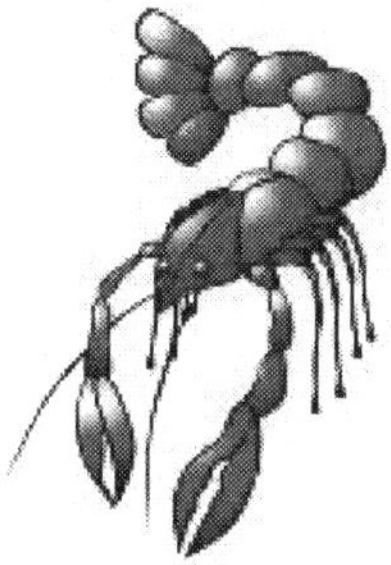

CHAPTER TWENTY TWO: Gettin' Back On Da Job

Back to Work

Well da weatha finally improve some an' da break time is all ova. Dere ain' no excuses left. Dis mornin' I gotta crank up da pickup an' hie on back to da job. We lucky to have a contrac', lot o' folks lookin' fo' work an' not findin' none.

Knuckles gonna meet me on da job. He's bringin all da woodworkin' 'quipment an' we gonna duplicate some antebellum trimboards. Dis gonna be one fine ol' plantation house when me an' Knuckles get done wit' it.

Dat is, o' course, if Knuckles rememba to get his butt out o' da bed dis mornin'. He tipped a bunch o' col' ones las' night so I ain' so sure he'll rememba' to get up. Could-might have to roust him outta da rack. Might-could be that's da best ting to do.

On da other hand he gets fiesty when someone interrupts his *zzzzz*s.

Dere Ain' No Money

I'm tinkin' it was dat fella Kris Kristofferson wrote da song and his sweetie pie gal Rita Coolidge sung 'dere ain' no money in Sout' Carolina.' Dere 'pparently ain' none in Louisiana neither. TT an' his crew was in Dupree's place las' nite an' dey was all pretty glum. Dey didn't make da nut dis year.

TT say shrimp season is closin' tomorrow at sundown, He say dey been catchin' jumbos an' doin' pretty good lately what wit' da price o' diesel down. Trouble was, he say, dat fuel prices didn't drop quick 'nough. Almost five buck a gallon back in da summertime killed any hope o' real profit fo' da year.

TT say dat he been hearin' from Shrimper's Association guys from Nort' Carolina to Mississippi dat dere ain' none o' dem makin' any money. Cost too much to keep da trawlers on da wata what wit fuel an' ice prices an' dey ain' getting' a high enough pound price fo' da shrimp.

TT figgers shrimpin' juss one more American industry goin' down da drain. It's sad to see dat way of life goin' on by.

Dat's what I tink me.

Tings is Workin' Out Fo' Someone

Guy on da work crew says to me his wife ain' speakin' to him. Says his daughta run off an' got married. His boy got a job an' ain' spongin' on him dis month. His dog bit da mailman so he ain' gettin' no bills in da box.

He figures it mus' be dat voodoo workin' fo' a change.

Fallin' Off Da Gable

I fell off da roof an' bounce in da dusty yard o' da manor house we fixin'. I thought fo' sure dat I busted a buncha bones. Knuckles call 911 an' da ambalance come an' took me to da horsepistol.

Dey X-ray me an' it turn out dat I'm banged up some but dere ain' nuttin' busted. Sawbones order me home to bed an' he tell me stay dere fo' a coupla days.

Leavin' Knuckles to supervise da job has me worryin' some. Dat boy is a firs' rate woodworker, an a fine teacher, but him as da crew honcho, I don' know 'bout dat?

Still, what choice do I have, It's Knuckles or no one, so, no, I shouldn' worry. Just have to trust Knuckles will run da crew okay.

One plus to dis convalescin' is dat Colleen been poor babyin' me all day. Bring me gumbo, an' corn bread, an 'nanna puddin'. Las' nite it was a big bowl o' ice cream, strawberry an' caramel swirl. *Mmmmmmmm.*

Dat gal, she bein' a sweetie pie. She juss bring me a col' one.

I tink dat's nice is what I tink, me.

Cajun Healt' Insurance

It's a good ting I got hauled to Sain' Aimee. It's da Catlic horsepistol. Best ting is dat Fadda LeBlanc is on da board o' directors an' da horsepistol is needin' some renovatin' work done. Fadda say we can do some horse tradin' dat'll get my bill covered.What I fear is dat da good Fadda goin' to 'clude a weddin' in da horse tradin' terms. Me an' Colleen luv each odder, but we doan need no pushin' us into quick matrimony, no.

Da horsepistol bill goin' to get worked out, but I ain' lookin' forward to da EMS am-balance bill.

Could-might talk to Antoine DuPage. Antoine a shirttail cousin on my Mama's side and he's on da Parish council. Dere is a rumor dat da emergency vehicle garage need some shorin' up.

Could-might be *Antoine* can hep' work me a deal wit' da EMS folk. Might-could.

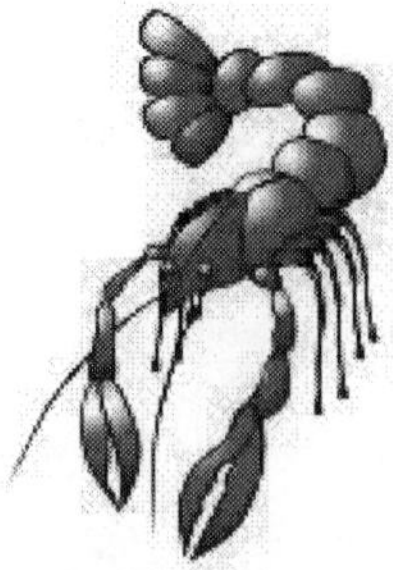

CHAPTER TWENTY THREE:
Knuckles Messin' Tings Up

Makin' Amends; Insurin' a Payday

Hurtin' or no, I gotta get back on da job. Knuckles was up on da roof finishin' off what I was workin' on before I took da dive. A big S-class Mercedes Benz pulled inta da driveway an a fine lookin' honey got outta dat car.

Knuckles took to hollerin' stuff like “Hot Momma” an' cruder stuff like, "nice rack." An' da crew picked up on da vulgarities. I wasn't dere to stop 'em an' from all dat I heard dey was 'bout outta control. Wasn't nice at all an' I am ashamed.

Turn out da lady dey was hootin' an' hollerin' at was da plantation house owner an' she's hoppin' mad. She call Colleen threatenin' to cancel da contrac'.

Dat happens I doan what we gonna do. No contrac' plus dem barter jobs we committed to is likely to mean no food on da table. I can't have dat, no.

So, here I am wit' my aches an' pains on da job an' chewin' out da crew, 'specially Knuckles.

I got a call into da lady dey insulted, an' I sure hope I can sweet talk her into forgiveness. Maybe I should 'vite her to the *fais do-do* down to Dupree's place Friday nite. Or maybe dat ain' such a good idea.

I betta tink o' sumptin' to make da lady happy. Dat's what I'm tinkin', me.

Apologizin'

I got through on da phone to da lady. Lemme tell you my knees was wobblin' trying to tink o' da right words to say to her. But, I managed. I tol' da lady dat I was sorry for da crew's crude an' rude behavior an' dat I chewed every one o' dem out. Promised her dat insults from da crew won't never happen no secon' time.

Da lady accepted my 'pology an' I took a gamble an' 'vited her to da Friday nite *fais do-do*. She said she ain' never been an' she accepted da invite.

I ain' so sure on my part how smart a move dat invite was an' neither is Colleen. Tomorrow will tell da story. Keepin' fingers crossed, me.

Laissez Le Bon Temps Rouler

If any o' you been wonderin' da answer is no, Colleen an' me we ain' set no date to get hitched yet. Dat fac' is givin' Fadda LeBlanc fits.

I had to sit Colleen down an' convince her to let it pass. I tol' her da priest, her cousin, ain' no busybody, it's just dat he worries 'bout our immortal souls. Dat's his job.

I tol' dat sweet Colleen dat as long as we know we ain' sinners den it doan matter none what no one else tinks an' dat includes da priest and da busy ol' hen wimmens what live an' gossip here in *Pigeonaire*.

Colleen juss nodded.

Me, I ain' sure Colleen truly believes what I been sayin'. I'm convinced dat deep down Colleen do worry 'bout what odders are tinkin' an' mouthin'. But, dere's nothin' I can do 'bout dat.

All I can do, an' it's all anybody can do, is ignore other folks opinions an' live life as I see it. An', of course, livin' down here in the Bayou country like we do we just got to *laissez le bon temps rouler*.

Tonite We Party

We all down to Dupree's place getting' ready for the Friday nite *soiree*. Rene, Dupree's olda brudder is cookin' up a bunch a pork butts fo' da bar-be-que. TT makin tater salad an' slaw. I'm doin' a bunch a boil shrimp an' makin a hot sauce fo' dippin' 'em in. Alla da lady's in town is whippin' up dere specialties, stuff like dirty rice an' jambalaya, an' seafood gumbo; lots of 'em are bakin' sweets.

We got a lot o' longnecks in da iced tubs. I'm wondering, me; does da lady from da plantation house drink beer? If she don't Dupree says he got anyting anybody might want on da back bar. So, I guess dere ain't nuttin' to worry 'bout.

Dupree say just go wit' da flow. But it ain't Dupree's contract I'm worring 'bout, it's mine.

Tink I betta get a cold beer, me.

Colleen say I betta count da col' ones. Could-might be good advice.

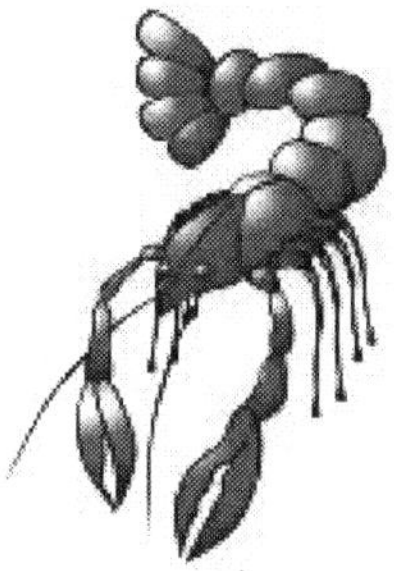

CHAPTER TWENTY FOUR: Maybe Tings Ain' So Bad

Plantation Lady

Turns out da turnout to Dupree's place las' nite was juss fine. Pretty much da whole town was dere an' we had us a time. I was a liddle nervous when Knuckles an' da crew showed up. I was more dan a liddle nervous when da lady from da plantation house show up.

Da fiddler and da Allemans accordian palyer got tings rollocking, startin' off wit' Jo-El Sonnier's version of *J'Etais au Bal* (I was in the ballroom) and keeping on wit' one afta 'nother Cajun favorite. Knuckles ask da plantation lady to dance an' I tought dat's all she wrote' concerning any chance we'd still have a contrac' come Monday.

I got real upset when Knuckles nuzzle da lady's ear an' she turn scarlet red. Den she start to laugh an seemed to be havin' a time wit' Knuckles. Turn out da lady was captivated when Knuckles whispa *chérie* in her ear.

Dey hit it off someting teriffic, 'specially when Knuckles 'pologize fo' his earlier behavior.

Dis mornin' Knuckles come by an' tell me da lady, her name is Catherine, is gonna rewrite da contrac' an' give us a whole buncha 'dditional work. Knuckles said him an' da lady are going to dinner at *Galitoire*'s in N'Awlins tonight. Looks like dey could-might be becomin' a item.

Seems like tings turnin' out good on da Bayou. But, I still got a problem. I was nervous las' nite an' dat got me to downin' too many 'col' ones. An', I must admit, I took me some o' dat Black Jack. Got knee walkin' drunk.

Colleen din't like dat one bit an' so now she's mad. Seems a body can't win.

Frettin' fo' Nuttin'

I worried an' fretted all the day long, dreadin' facin' up to my Sweetie. Knuckles try to get me to take a slug or two o' dat Tennessee sour mash to calm my nerve, but I said no, ain' goin' dat route no mo', no.

Dupree buck me up some by tellin' how sweet Colleen is but he ain' neva dealt wit dat woman when she got her mad on.

Fadda LeBlanc didn't help at-tall, he jes' chuckle ova my 'dickament.

It turn out dat all my worries was fo' naught. I brung a buncha deep red roses an' I guess dat Colleen guess I was gonna do sumptin' like dat. She had a big ol' vase already at the ready.

I tell dat sweet woman I was bad an' wrong an' that I'm one sorry Bayou boy.

She jes' stan' dere wit her arms folded an' a frown on her angel face.

I thought I would neva get back in her good grace.

But, den she smile an' I knew da trouble was ova. We kiss an' make up an' bes' of all she pull her gold chain off, open da clasp, an' drop da key to dat Harley I been admirin' in my han'.

Couldn't hardly believe what was happenin'.

All's well now, especially afta da fine makeup meal we share at the Café Vermilionville in Layfayette.

Tomorrow Colleen is goin' wit' me to pick up the new Harley an' we goin' away for da weekend. Me, I'm one happy Cajun boy.

Dat's what I am, me.

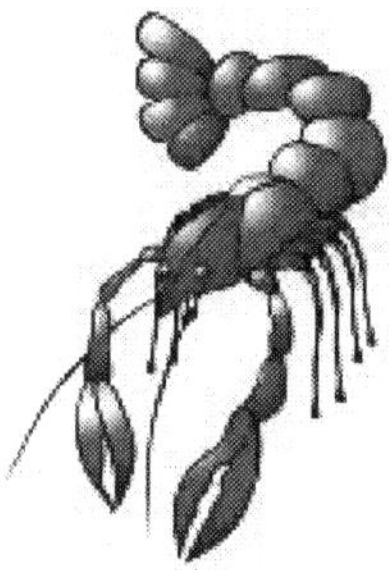

CHAPTER TWENTY FIVE:
Comin' Storms

Dis Year

Da hurricane season is soon upon us again. Sure do hope us Bayou folk doan get hammered 'gain dis year. But, worrin' won't get me nowhere. We live in da Hurricane zone an' we gotta expect trouble sometimes. Just gotta cope.

An' dat's da troof.

Da Fish Warden

Wit da springtime come da fish warden an' dere ain' nothin' in da world dat Cajun boys like less. But it's da dumb politicians keep changin' da laws an' da warden get da dirty work of enforcin. It's easy to hate dem wardens, but dat's wrong.

Cajun boys, like my frien' TT Fontenot know mo' dan da politicians up to Baton Rouge an' dere ain' nothing dose boys would do to harm da shrimp an' fish dat mak' dem their livin'. But Cajun boys also know dat da law cut off da shrimp season too soon. Dey know dat da spawnin' populations wouldn't be hurt by a coupla weeks more shrimpin'. So, da boys poach some, not too much, juss some.

Was a time wardens would issue citations with fines fo' getting' caught at da poachin'. Cajun boys was okay with dat, but now da law been changed an' da wardens grab da boat an' dat puts dem shrimp poachers out o' bidness.

Some o' da hot head young Shrimper boys want to shoot da wardens, but older wiser heads won't let dem do dat. Even though they doan like enforcement by confiscation dose older guys know da wardens ain' to blame fo' bad laws. Politicians are da culprits.

Da older men counsel dat da Shrimpers an' Fishers Association gotta get stronger and fight for fair an' proper conservation laws. Me, I'm a carpenter not a fisher or a shrimper but I agree wit' da older men.

Now Da Early Storm

We all gonna be heading out fo' south-west Louisiana, down dere near on to da Texas border. Da folks down dere was hit hard by dis latest storm what blew in from da Gulf. Mos o' dem folk dat live between Lake Charles an' da Sabine pass ain' got much money. Dey hurtin' an' dey need a hand.

We got da pickups loaded wit' tools an' da trailers are piled high wit' lumba', an windows, an' blue tarps, an' odder roofin' materials.

Knuckles rounded up da work crews an' Colleen organized a food drive here in Pidgeonaire. We got plenty o' construction goods an' plenty o' good vittles to haul to dem folk.

Be hittin' da road soon to bring dem folk what need it some help.

Doin' Da Tawkin'

Seen' as how da storm was still ragin' an' we couldn't get on da road yesterday me an' Colleen had dat talk 'bout da future.

We 'greed dat neither one o' us is ready for da big step but we ain' sayin' it ain't never goin' to happen neither. I had da 'gagement ring in my pocket an' I tried to give it to her. She said no, not yet. She tinks dat maybe I should take da ring back to where I bought it an' I'm thinkin' on dat. Could-might be better if I put da ring in a safe deposit box in da town bank, get it quick when I need it.

Knuckles just pulled up an give a honk on da horn, so it looks like it's time to get goin'. Soon as I give Colleen a goodbye kiss dat is.

Tings Happenin' On Da Bayou

We got back from sout' wes' Louisiana and den we got all da work all done on a big plantation house up to West Feliciana Parish. Da paycheck was a whoppa.

Me and dat beauty Colleen celebrated wit a weekend in N'Awlin's. Was nice, but kinda sad too. Several years have passed all-reddy an' da city ain' but a shell o' what it usta was. Dere ain' no crowds in da Quarta even though da floodin' didn't get dere.

Still me an' Colleen had us a time togetha. I ain' fillin' in none o' the details though.

We got back to Pigeonaire in time to get Knuckles back up to Angola for da big spring convict rodeo. Dat Knuckles has his pardon an' he ain' a convict no more, but he promise da Warden dat he'd come back and ride da bull an' da buckin' horse one las' time. He not only done dat, he won da big ol' All Roun' Cowboy buckle.

Lemme tell you, Knuckles, he was one beamin' proud Cowboy, dat boy was.

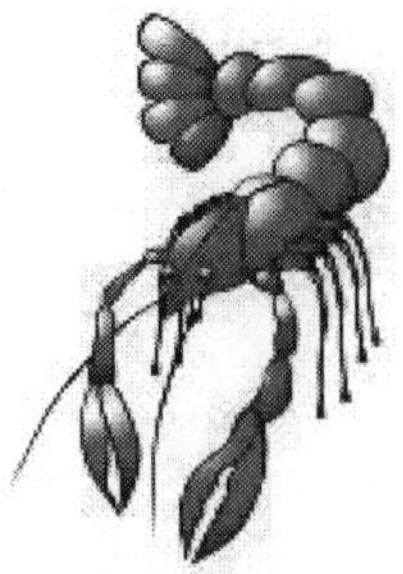

CHAPTER TWENTY SIX:
Da Meat Locka

Pig Party

We plannin' a big *fête* down to Duprees' roadhouse soon. Da whole nine yard. Pig roast, crawfish boil, an da cookoff contest wit da file gumbo, jambalaya, *etouffe*, crawfish pie, fry catfish, an' all sortsa odder Cajun dishes. Dere's gonna be table o' different kinds o' sweets, but 'specially da scrumptious *gateaux* da wimmen so good at bakin'.

We gonna have us a party. Dat's what I say, me.

Missin' Body

Dere's a sadness on the *Teche* dis mornin'. A mournin'. An' dere's anger. Dis town suffa a great loss ova night. Enough to get us all riled.

Da boys was getting' ready for da *fais do-do* at da party yard down to Dupree's place. Dey got da bar-be-que pit all clean out an re-dug. Da picnic tables all scrub down wit soapy wata an' stiff brushes. All da cook pots shiny clean.

Then dis mornin' we go downtown an' open up da meat locker at *LeGuin*'s meat market where da pig has been stored.

Da carcass is gone.

Dere's a empty meathook where da hog shoulda been hangin'.

Damn if it doan look like some bad boys broke in an' stole a hunnert an' fifty poun' pig. Had to get us a secon' hog dis time, seein' as how da firs' one was stole. Lemme tell you, dere's some upset Cajuns in dis town. We find out who stole da pig dere's gonna be a major pummeling.

An' dat ain' da first word o' no lie, no siree, I guarantee.

B-B-Q Pig

Fixin' da pig ain' hard, provided you got some big guys an' a supply o' col' ones. An' providin' da pig ain' been stole.

Firs' we get a hunnert-fifty poun' pig from da butcha shop, lean one dat won' start no grease fir'. Buttafly dat pig da day before an rub him wit da dry spice. Den da nex' day lay him out on da pit grate fo' da cookin'.

Gotta mak' da fire in advance. We use `bout tree-four big bags o' charcoal briquettes an mak' da fire nex' to da pit so we can move da coals to da pit as we need `em. We add coals to da pit all da day long. Mak' sure dem coals is all `long da sides o' da pit wit' extra ones on da ends.

Cook da hog fo' ten-twelve hour. You wanna cook skin up fo' 6-8 hours. Den fo' two hour or so on da flip side. Finish cooking wit da skin up again. Watch da temperature wit a good meat thermometer stuck in one o' da hams. When it get to 170 degrees on da F scale da hog is cooked.

You gonna need a mop sauce to baste da hog every hour or so. An B-B-Q sauce fo' when da pig just `bout finish.

When da hog is done pull him from da fir' an' wrap him in foil. Let him set an hour or so den start pullin' da meat. Cleaver up da hog into large chunks, `bout 5 to 10 pounds a piece. Den pull da meat, mixing' it from all parts o' da pig an' put it in a large pot fo' serving' from.

Da secret to a good pig is havin' da boys to watch da fire all day an' all nite to make' sure da carcass doan burn none.

Dat's all dere is to it.

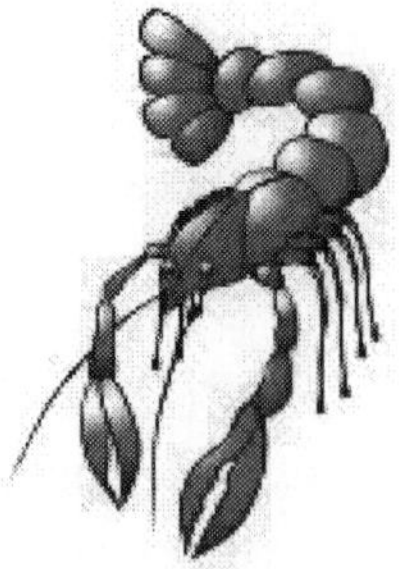

CHAPTER TWENTY SEVEN: Ain Gettin' Da Work

Da News Ain' Good

Las' night we et da pig wit' some *étouffée* dat Dupree's brudda Rene cook and it was scrumptious good. Trouble was dat, except fo' da pulled pig an' some odder fixin's, dat *étouffée* was 'bout da onliest good ting 'bout Friday nite.

We got us news an' it weren't good.

Colleen say she spent her day goin' ova da books an' it look like we headin' fo' trouble. Seems dat folks what want us to do restoration work on dey plantation homes is passin' on our work proposals right an' left.

Ain' our fault an' it ain' theirs, neither. It's da banks refusin' to len' dem folks da money dey need. Dey doan get money we doan get contracts fo' da work.

Been a carpenta all my life but I'm new to bidness ownin' gig an' dis stuff 'bout da economic downturn hurtin' da bidness is all new to me. Usta was I juss got layed off. Now I have to do da layin' off. Dat ain' fun.

Me an' my sweetie gonna have to put da tinkin' cap on an' figure how to weatha dis rough patch. *Hoo-wee*, I neva figured bidness bein' dis complex.

I dunno, now we got annuder storm forcast an' we on uncharted wata wit trin' to keep da bidness up an' goin'.

Dat's da tings what I'm worrin' about, me.

Da Time Ain' Right

Colleen say no suga tonite.

She sayin' dat da time ain' right fo' foolin' 'roun. Says we gotta knuckle down, get serious, an' figger us a plan to weatha dis credit crunch.

I tol' her it ain' no worry, dem contracts will come back when da banks free up da money. Meantime, I say dat da family own a big plot up in da Dismal Swamp in Virginia an' dere's plenty preserved first growth pine logs back here.

My uncle Pete has a sawmill dat he ain' usin no more. Pete also got a ol' eighteen wheela dat Knuckles an' I can use to fetch dat heart pine. We can change our bidness fo' a while. Manufacture floorin' an' sell it to Home Depot or Lowes.

Colleen say dat just might be a plan. Den she ask where in da worl' we gonna get da money fo' gassin' dat ol' eighteen wheeler.

Dere's allas some fly in da ointment. But, we'll find a way, dat's what I figger, me.

I wonda if now I can figger da same way 'bout dat suga?

Da Sawmill An' Da Log Truck

Me an' Knuckles got ova to uncle Pete's sawmill dis mornin' an' look ova da 'quipment. Everything seem to be in pretty good repair

Dere's an big ol' plank cuttin' saw dat's in workin' orda. An' a planer an' a millin' machine fo' smoothin out da boards an cutting tongue an groove. Pete took good care o' dat 'quipment an' when he lay it up he make sure da working' parts was grease coated. Dat's a good ting.

Da eighteen wheeler is an ol' Bulldog Mack from back in da sixties wit' a big long log haulin' trailer. Da tires good an' truck run okay but she leakin' oil some. Knuckles an' me got some gasket replacin' work to do before we run on up to Virginia.

Looks like we can get underway in a day or so. But firs' I gotta find out who has title to dat swamp lan'. I been tol' my Daddy owned it, but one don't eva know for sure lessen one checks. Now, I gotta figger out where da deed might be put.

Maybe lawyer *Pettibone*'ll know. Dat lawyer an my Daddy was thick. Hope he don't charge a fee fo' askin'.

Dat's what I hope, me.

Hittin' Da Road

We got dat ol' diesel tracta fixed up good, no oil leakin' no mo', an' we got da rest o' our stuff in Knuckles pick-em-up an on da flatbed utility trailer. I'll be drivin' da big rig an' Knuckles pullin' da utility trailer wit da tools an' da winch an' da log chains fo' yankin' dem preserved pines from da boggy mud.

Colleen come up wit enough money fo' da trip north an' back. Right now we all is headin' fo' Dupree's place fo' a coupla col' ones an' oysta Po-boys. Den some early shuteye so's we can get on da road before daybreak.

Colleen an uncle Pete got an idea fo' reclaimin ol' cypress wood from buildings wrecked by dem storms, Katrina an' Rita an' Ike. My sweetie an' my uncle gonna work out da details while Knuckles an' me are up to Virginia. Colleen say we can do da work on profit shares so we won't have to lay out no cash.

I tink we gonna weatha dis construction downturn.

Dat's what I'm prayin' happens, me.

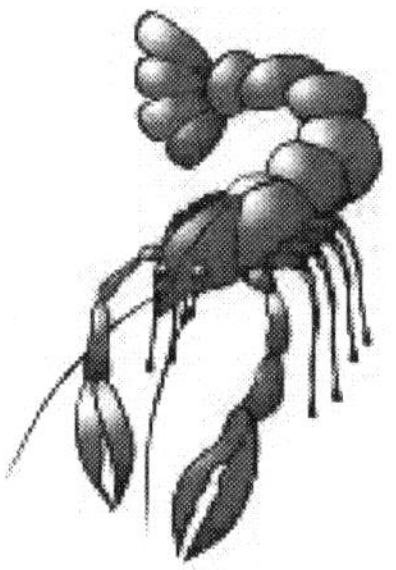

CHAPTER TWENTY EIGHT:
Da Trip Nort'

Colleen Gonna Have Her A Hissy Fit

Dang, not even outta da State yet, me an' dere's a blue light flashin' Colleen gonna have a fit if dis cost us money. We can't' 'fford takin' a hit.

Betta pull da rig ova an face da music

Dat cop walkin' up to my tracta-traila look awful stern in his Stetson an' dem dark shades. Betta not give him no argument, no.

Dere go Knuckles flyin' roun' my tracta-traila. Man's grinning' like a big ol' ape.

He's gonna get a piece o' my min' when we hook up. Dere ain' a single thing dat's funny 'bout what's happenin' here, no.

Getting' Away

Crossed da border safe into Mississippi now an' I spot Muscles' pick-em-up an' traila in a truckstop diner up ahead. Bit o' breakfast would taste good 'bout now, so I tug da rig's wheel hard right an' roll on inta da parkin' lot.

Inside dere's Muscles sittin' in a booth. He got dat same grin on as when da cop pull me ova an' he run on past da scene o' da infraction.

I slip into da booth an' Muscles ask, "dat ol' boy give you a ticket?"

I say, "no. Da cop was walkin' toward my rig an' he stop. Den he turn 'roun, get back in da cruisa, an' he take off. Doan know what dat was 'bout, but I doan care neither, I put da rig in gear an' skedaddle toward da borda."

Muscles bust out laughin' an' he say, "I called da State police barracks on up da road. Tol' da dispatcha dere was a terrible pile up back toward Alexandria. I figga your cop got da call an' he decide dat's mo' important dan givin' you a ticket. Figgered right, I reckon."

What dat boy Knuckles done was some big time breakin' o' da law but I bust out laughin' anyway. "You done dat," I say, "you sure done dat."

Headin' Home

Knuckles an' me, we got to da Great Dismal Swamp an' pulled a big load o' them preserved pine logs. We hustlin' dem back to Louisiana now. Cuttin' an' smoothin' dem to floor boards is da next task fo' us.

Knuckles called his gal, dat rich lady Catherine, an' tol' her 'bout foolin' da State cop. He say dey had a good laugh 'bout dat.

Den, dat gal call Colleen and Colleen get me on da cell phone. *Hoo-boy*, she was fumin'. Say Knuckles could get throwed back in Angola fo' makin' a false police report. She chew me out like it was my doin'.

Me, I said dat what Knuckles done wit da State cops worked fo' me. I'm grateful fo' havin' dodged a expensive ticket. Another ting is it wasn't me what made da false report.

I did have to 'gree wit' Colleen dat Knuckles ain' always da brightest bulb in da chandelier. But, he always means well an' his callin' da police barracks sho' nuff helped me out of a jam. Dat boy is my good frien' an' I said dere's no way I was gonna sit still fo' her bad moutin' him, her kin or no.

We argue back an forth fo' a while till Colleen admitted dat she wasn't all dat mad she was juss worried. I tol' her dat I worry too sometime, but Knuckles always does what seem to him to be da right ting. An' dat to me ain't a worse way to operate. Dat ended our back an' forth 'bout Muscles's behavior.

Colleen tol' me dat she an' uncle Pete set up a buncha deals fo' reclaimin' Cypress lumba. Lawyer *Pettibone* draw up da contracts an he agree to wait fo' his fee 'till da contract money start rollin' in. Looks like we in bidness.

All in all, tings might be lookin' up.

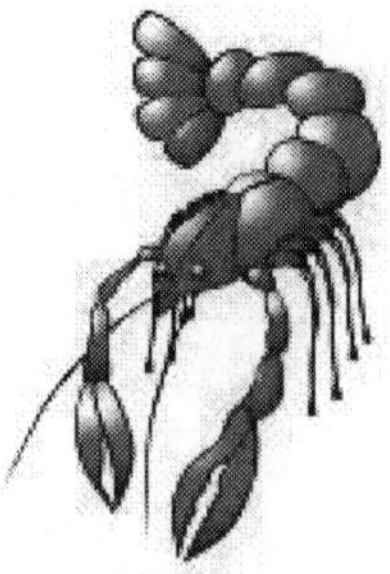

CHAPTER TWENTY NINE: Tinkin' On Gettin' Hitched

Dere's A Bad Wind Blowin'

It comin' in on Terrebonne parish dis mornin' wit da hurricane winds drivin' da rain. We up here in *Sain' Martin* parish battenin' da hatches to ride out dis storm. Da lumba yard run outta plywood sheets yesterday an' dere ain' a generator to be had at da Home Depot, but we 'bout ready as can be for da comin' storm.

Dere ain' nuttin' else much to do but 'vacuate or hunker down an' pray. Hunkerin' down is our way, 'vacuatin' ain't..

We got ta pray too fo' N'Awlins; dey doan need dem levees breached one mo' time, no.

Buttaflys

Hoo-boy, dat hurricane turnin' an still might be comin' out o' Cuba an' headin' dis way, but now it seem da chances are slimmin' down. Dat's good 'cause odder tings is on my mind. I'm gonna have to bite da bullet on dis weddin' proposal ting.

I been tinkin' on what to do all las' night an I'm still tinkin' dis mornin'.

Dere ain' nothin' to do but do da right ting by dat sweet gal o' mine. I know she was okay with puttin' tings off, but dat can't go on fo' eva. Still, doin' da right ting doan mean I ain' nervous; no sir, it doan mean dat at-all.

Dis aftanoon I can slip away from da job an' get da 'gagement ring from da safe deposit box. Maybe put some *Champagne* on ice.

I ain' a bit sure 'bout what Colleen's answer gonna be when I ask her 'bout settin' da date.

Whole ting got me worried. My stomach is flyin' buttaflys.

In Our Cypress Bayou Home

We had da repast down to Dupree's place. Colleen says she'll tink hard on settin' a date. We back home now. Doin' a liddle kissin' an' huggin' an', who knows what else, maybe.

Den we're going to get us a good solid night o' sleep. No worries. No nightmares. Juss some fine good zzzzzs.

We gotta lot o' work to get at in da mornin' an' we gonna be fresh to get at it.

G'nite now.

Da Weekend Ova

Knuckles an' me, we doin' more clean up-fix up dis week. Da weekend back home was a fine time. We had us a big ol' crawfish boil down to Dupree's place an' mos of da town come. Dat *écrevisse* was scrumptious. *Mmmm*, suckin' out dem mudbug heads is one fine treat. But work is where it is now.

Gotta go, da crew is hollerin' an' fightin' 'bout what to do next. I never figured dat da boss man was gonna have to spend so much time straightenin' da boys out an' tellin' them what's on da platter.

But, I'm da boss man an' dat's what I got to do, me.

Workin'

Me an' Knuckles an' Colleen had us a good week fo' a change. Got some stuff done. Got some contracts paid. Paid the crew. Had dollars left over. Was a good week.

Now we can kick back, some.

Gonna Have Us A Time

Friday nite come an' Colleen an me went ova to Dupree's place for da oysta roast. *Mmmmm*, dem Gulf oystas was good.

Evrabody was happy dat me an' my sweetie is on good terms. TT calls it kissy-face, but TT always been a smart-alec.

We takin da motacycles dis morning an' goin' to Galveston fo' da rest of da weekend. Gonna have us a time, Colleen an' me. Yeah, we gonna do dat, fo' sure.

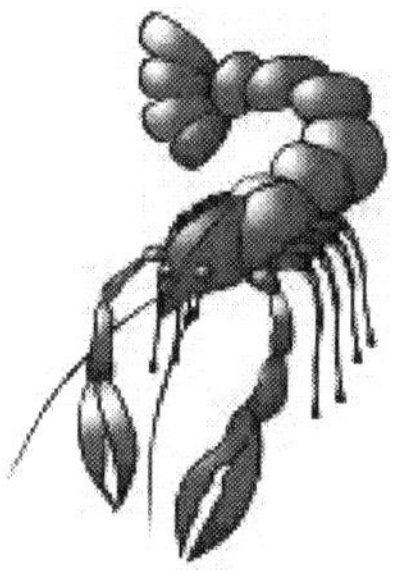

CHAPTER THIRTY:
Off To Galveston

Motacycle Trip

Was a long ride to Galveston, betta than two hunnret an' fifty miles. Me an' Colleen fire up da bikes Saddaday mornin' an' get on da road. We was flyin' mos' o' da time, doin' eighy, sometimes ninety miles a hour. *Whooee*, 'zilleratin', dat was what it was.

We was goin' south on Texas eighty-seven by 'bout noon. Dat's da gulf highway dat go to da ferry to Galveston. Man, 'bout fifty or sixty bikes come outta nowhere an' join up wit' Colleen an' me. Tough lookin' buncha bikers, tootin horns an' wavin' power fists. Anyways, we were getting' low on gas an' we pull into a roadhouse/gas station.

Da whole flock o' bikers ride on into da parkin; lot wit' us. Dey shoutin' an' revvin' engines an' makin' all kinda noise. Coupla big guys start circling Colleen an' me an' I was getting' nervous, worrin' dat I was gonna have to defend my gal's honor wit dis tough bunch. Dat happen', it's gonna be a nasty situation.

Dat's what I figga, me.

Da Peace-maker

Colleen kick her bike stand down, jump offa da machine, an' wave da leader o' da motacycle bunch ova to where she standin'. She smiles an' says sumptin'.

I can't hear but da next ting I know is da guy gives some sorta signal and all o' da gang parks their bikes. Dey comes ova laughin' an' jokin', nice like, wit' Colleen an me.

Da motacycle boys turn out to be a fine bunch o' interestin' guys. Tol' us a lot 'bout da Texas gulf coast. Some o' dem boys join us fo' lunch an' we had us a fine time. Not only dat, dey picked up da check.

We finished lunch, gassed up, and said goodbye to our new friends an' hit da road. We got into Galveston 'bout mid-afternoon an' check into da hotel. We're gonna go out an' look ova dis town in a few minutes.

All I can say is my sweetie is one piece o' work. One minute I thought we was in big trouble, da nex' moment we got us a buncha new friends.

Dat Colleen is one amazin' gal.

An' me, I'm one lucky ol' Louisiana boy.

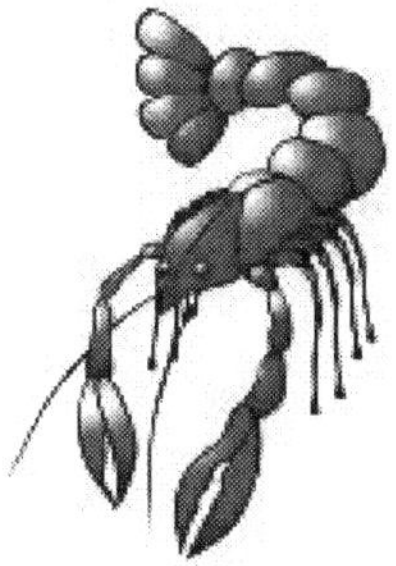

CHAPTER THIRTY ONE:
Back In Pigeonaire

She Got Me All Confuse

Colleen an' me, we back from Texas an' I'm on da way to da job dis Monday mornin'. On da way I got me in some trouble an' got hauled off to the horsepistol once again. Colleen come to check on me but she had to wait some as dere was Louisiana State Troopers in da room servin' me a summons. Seems dey measure da brake marks on da road an' figger I was drivin' da pickup ova a hunnert miles an' hour when I dump it in da Bayou.

Anyhoo when dem cops leave Colleen say I was irresponsible drivin' da pick-em-up like dat. She say she gonna have to tink hard before she give me da answer on da date settin' fo' our weddin'. Says maybe I been provin' dat I ain' a grown up 'nough man fo' da matrimony. She ask me to keep the ring 'til she make up her mind.

I doan know why it should take so much time to make up her mind. I'm a handsome fellow. I got a good bidness. I ain't neva cheated on her. An' I can be a lotta fun.

Dem's my good points an' to my way o' tinkin' dey should be 'nough.

Da Priest Again

Fadda LeBlanc come by afta Colleen's visit. He 'greed wit' me 'bout da good points. It's da not growin' up an' bein' responsible parts dat he think could-might get in the way some. Da priest says he understan' why a woman might worry 'bout lack of maturity. When da chiren come da *Maman* gotta take care o' da basics but da *Papa* gotta set da example o' growin' up right.

Maybe da Fadda's on to sumptin' but it's my life an' no wife gonna tell me I can't go an' have me some fun. Besides, I doan tink drivin' da pickup fast is irresponsible. Dat's why dey put in da big motors an' dat's why da speedo say 140 mph at da peg. Drivin' da truck a liddle fast is juss me bein' me, like I is meant to be. Dat's all.

Gettin' Sprung Dis Mornin'

I'm feelin' real good, my haid doan hurt, an' I'm getting' sprung from the horsepistol dis mornin'. Da Docs checked me out good an' dey say da knock on my hard head ain' caused no permanent damage. Colleen say she ain' so sure 'bout dat.

Tomorrow we gonna be packin' da pickups wit' tools, an' generators an' pumps, an coolers o' shrimp an' other good stuff to eat. Soon's we know where da hurricane hit we'll head on out to lend a hand wit' da cleanup. Looks like we'll be goin' toward Houston or Galveston again, mos' likely Lake Charles on da Louisiana side.

Dat remind me, I ain'got a pickup no mo', me. Gonna have to hie on ova to da dealer dis afternoon an' get me a new one. Maybe dat black four door F-150 wit' da Harley Davison option package dat I've had my eye on fo' a bit. Dat's some nice truck.

Gas is high an' some folks is advisin' me to get a compac' pickup. But dem' folks doan know dat convertin' to compressed natural gas fo' fuel is easy, 'specially here in oil/gas country. We all know how to do da conversion to our trucks. Get dat compressed gas at da wellhead fo' free. Gonna be burned off as a waste product otherwise.

When we get back from da hurricane cleanup me an' Colleen gonna have to sit down an' have us annuder serious talk. Things 'tween us gotta get settled.

Dat's what has to be.

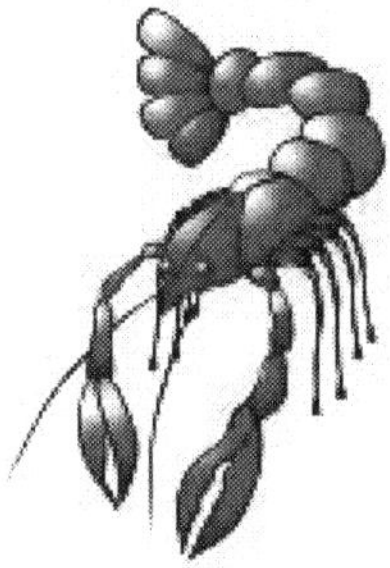

CHAPTER THIRTY TWO:
Tings Lookin' Up

It's Gettin' Betta Again

We been back in Pigeonaire fo' a while now an' things is improvin'. Dis Saddaday Dupree's olda brudder, Rene, is cookin' *écrevisse.* Da ladies are bringin' dere favorite dishes to complement da crawfish boil. Dere's gonna be more than plenty o' col' ones on da ice.

What, you ask, is da reason for dis fête dis time?

Well, I tell you why, me. We finally seen da last o' da FEMA trailers dragged outta our home town. Everyting is rebuilt or fixed up like it usta was. Dere ain't no remmnant o'either Katrina or Rita or Ike to remin' us o' da bad times we suffa after dem hurricanes. We can be celebratin' now.

Yesiree things is lookin' up on da Bayou once mo'. We feelin' good an' feelin' good is reason we're gonna have us a time.

Dat's what I say, me.

Da Deal's Done Done

Me an Colleen finally agreed dat we're gonna hitch up an' we set da date in our minds. She took da ring an' we got congratulations from evera-one. Fadda LeBlanc ask when he can start 'nnouncin' da banns. Colleen tol' him not jus' yet. Da good priest pull a puss but he nodded an' we took it to mean he understan' even if he ain't too happy.

Right now we're juss gonna party. Da Cajun way. We gonna: *Laissez Le Bon Temps Rouler*

RECIPES

SOME IS CAJUN, AND SOME AIN'T

The recipes that follow are a few good things that I and my friends like to cook and eat. They are for the most part informal guides open to experiment, adaption, customization. The amounts listed in ingredients are not precise because that's the way I like to cook, a pinch of this, a handful of that. Maybe a dollop of something, or a shake from the container or several grinds of the salt or pepper grinder.

I thought about a formal arrangement for the recipes presented, starting with appetizers and ending with desserts. But, I decided that's the common way, not my way. Better, I think, for the reader to peruse the recipes and find what appeals. So, the recipes that you find here are arranged in no particular order. They are just there, put down in print as they came to me. But, they're good. They're tasty. I cook them and I eat them. So do my friends. I hope you will too.

Thumb through the offerings. Find what you might like. Cook it. Eat it. Change it. Adapt to your palate. Mostly enjoy.

Bon Appetit

Cajun Cooking Basics

For Cajun cooking the first thing is to make a brown roux. Here's how.

Roux:

One cup of vegetable oil
One cup of white flour in a sifter
Some salt an' some pepper

The recipe can be cut in half or in quarters if you like.

Heat the oil real hot and sprinkle in some salt an' cracked black pepper. Now, cut the heat to medium an' slowly add the flour from the sifter while stirring constantly. Continue stirring until the roux turns a rich dark brown and there is a nutty smelling flavor. Remove from the heat.

It takes 'bout a half hour of constant stirring to be sure that the roux doesn't burn. Rule 1: Throw the roux out an start again if it does burn.

When the roux is ready take a break and have yourself a cold beer or a sip of wine.

Use as much roux as needed for whatever you are cooking. The rest can be stored in the refrigerator for a few days.

Here's a quick way to make a roux:

one cup of flour
one cup of good oil
Mix together in a Pyrex bowl. Microwave on high for six minutes. Stir. Cook on high for another 30 seconds to a minute until the Roux is a dark brown.

Add the Trinity:

Now for just about any Cajun dish you can stir the sautéed trinity into the roux (chopped onion, chopped celery, and chopped green bell pepper).

Sauté the trinity in an oil butter mix on high for three minutes. Add some chopped green onion, several cloves of minced garlic. Sauté another 2 minutes. Stir in enough hot water to bring the roux up to a four cup (32 oz.) measure. Result: A smooth dark microwaved roux with veggies in about 12 minutes.

The Trinity:

Indispensable vegetables for Cajun cooking. Onion. Celery. Green Pepper. Dice them fine. Sauté them. Use them in darn near everything.

Essential Cajun Sausages:

Andouille, frequently associated with Cajun cookin' Andouille is used in making jambalaya, étouffée, gumbo and the like, but it's good in lots of other dishes and by itself. It's a sausage of coarse-grained smoked pork, pepper, onions, and seasonings. The pork used often comes from smoked Boston Butt. Once it's casing is stuffed, the sausage is re-smoked. The result is delicious. Most super markets carry Andouille.

Boudin is sausage generally made of cooked rice, pork, pork liver, onion, green bell pepper, and seasonings stuffed in a casing. There are variations such as seafood boudin, alligator boudin, and crawfish boudin.

I think Boudin is great when roasted with whole okra pods. Spray the sausage and okra with olive oil and roast at 400 degrees for a few minutes (until they begin to brown). Make sure the caps and stems are not removed from the okra pods (that keeps them from becoming slimy).

Tasso isn't rightly a sausage but it's often used in Cajun cooking along with sausages and is a great compliment. Tasso is a smoked seasoning meat used to flavor dishes Cajun gumbo, red beans and rice, jambalaya and other stuff. It's a lean chunk of cured pork (usually shoulder) or beef that's been richly seasoned with ingredients such as red pepper, garlic, file' powder and any of several other herbs or spices. It's then smoked for about 2 days. The result is a firm, smoky and flavorful tangy meat that is principally used for seasoning. Originally Tasso came from trim after an Acadian Hog Boucherie, thin strips were heavily seasoned, dried, then smoked for hours. These days however, most of the Tasso that is available is more like ham than the old style. Tasso will keep in the freezer.

Tasso can be purchased in gourmet stores or on the internet, use it as the search keyword.

Or make your own Tasso.

My friend Rick Stone owns and operates the Beaufort Baking Company, a bakery/restaurant, on Lady's Island SC.

Here's friend Rick's Tasso recipe:

Tasso:

5 Lb Pork butt
21 oz. Kosher Salt
11 oz. Sugar
3 Tbs. Pink Salt (Insta Cure #1)
1 Tbs. White Pepper

1 tsp. Cayenne Pepper
1 tsp Marjoram
1 tsp. Allspice

Trim pork butt into strips about 1 inch by1 inch by 6 inches long.

Thoroughly coat the meat in salt, sugar and pink salt. Let sit in refrigerator for 4-5 hours, tossing twice.

Rinse off the salt mixture and pat the meat dry. Coat in remaining spices and smoke in a smoker until internal temperature reaches 150 degrees.

Cool the meat and enjoy fresh for about a week, or wrap the individual slices and freeze for up to a month. Great stuff to liven up your Cajun dishes.

TABASCO® brand Pepper Sauce

There must be hundreds of different brands of hot pepper sauces, but as far as I'm concerned the McIlhenny Company TABASCO brand Pepper Sauce is the only one. The brand is a Louisiana specialty that's always found in Cajun kitchens and on Cajun dining tables. Cajun cooks find it indispensable even though the best of those cooks use Tabasco sauce sparingly, preferring to let the diner add to taste at the table.

Tabasco sauce is essential to Cajun food. It goes in Gumbos, in etouffees, in Jambalya, in stews and soups, and in just about anything Cajun. Tabasco sauce is also great with many other foods and cooking styles.

McIlhenny Company on Avery Island, La has been making and aging, and bottling their Tabasco original sauce since 1868. They grow their own special hot peppers and make a mash for the sauce. The pepper mash used for Tabasco sauce is aged for up to three years in white oak barrels.The mash is blended with distilled vinegar and salt to make the sauce. The resulting Tabasco sauce is plenty hot at about 2,500-5,000

Scoville heat units. Other pepper sauces may be hotter but, in my opinion, they are not better.

If you're gonna cook and eat Cajun food you must have Tabasco sauce. It's delicious on other stuff too, like for instance, scrambled eggs or in soups and stews. Tabasco sauce has no stabilizers or preservatives and it's possible that the sauce may separate. How the sauce is stored also has an effect on separation. That being said, a simple shake will typically bring the sauce and the solids back together. So, before using Tabasco sauce, give it a shake.

Try Tabasco sauce if you haven't. Enjoy it. Don't use too much or it might set your taste buds on fire.

Rice:

Rice goes with most anything. It's essential for most Cajun dishes.

A most basic rice recipe that everybody needs.
One cup of long grain white rice
One and three fourths cup of water (or chicken broth if you prefer)
One teaspoon salt

For larger amounts:
2 cups rice--3.25 water
3 cups rice-- 4 water
4 cups rice--5 water
5 cups rice--6 water
Adjust salt

Combine water, rice and salt and bring to a boil. Cover and simmer for 20-25 minutes. Check. It should be done. If not give it a few more minutes. Fluff with a fork and serve.

Alternatives are to use chicken or beef stock or tomato or V8 juice instead of water for cooking.

Bacon:

Buy good quality thin sliced bacon. Fry it crisp in a cast iron pan or griddle. A non-stick electric griddle also works. Always save the drippings for cooking many recipes.

Or, use the oven method:
Large baking sheet
Cover with crinkled up aluminum foil to help drain the bacon and catch the drippings
Place strips of bacon on the foil
Bake at 425 degrees for 20 minutes or until crisp
Remove the crisp bacon and save the drippings

Crisp bacon is great for breakfast, lunch, dinner, or supper. I love bacon with eggs, fried or scrambled. I love lettuce and tomato and crisp bacon on rye toast, salted and peppered and slathered with mayonnaise. I crumble and use bacon in several recipes, like the Heart Busting Beef Burgundy recipe presented later in this book.

Save the bacon drippings to use as cooking fat. It's great in many dishes.

Bacon is just good food. Hooray for bacon! Yummy!

Fatback:

Like bacon, the fat from a pigs back is essential to much of Southern cooking. It slices like bacon and is great asset to vegetable dishes like cabbage, green beans, collards, beans and lots of other stuff.

Get fatback in the grocery store.

Eggs:

Mostly chicken eggs, but occasionally other ones, like duck or turtle. We use them in all kinds of recipes, but what about eggs as just plain eggs. I like them scrambled. I like them fried.

Here's how I do them.

Scrambled Eggs:

Take a dozen eggs and crack them into a mixing bowl. Add salt, pepper, herbs (oregano, basil, rosemary), Greek or Creole seasoning to taste and a teaspoon or so of water. Maybe a drop or two of Tabasco sauce. Whip with a wire whisk. Cook on a hot griddle or frying pan slathered with bacon drippings. Turn the eggs until done but still moist.

Serve with crisp bacon, sausage, fried ham and with grits or fried potatoes.

Fried Eggs:

Two or three eggs a person. Drop them on a bacon drippings greased pan and fry until done, sunny side up, over easy, or cooked longer, your taste.

I like to add freshly ground black pepper and a Cajun or Creole spice mix to the eggs immediately after dropping them in the frying pan. But, that's up to you. Do 'em as you like 'em.

Whichever way they are cooked eggs are yummy.

And essential.

Buttered Toast:

No, no, not Wonder Bread, don't use it, it's tasteless, it's gummy, it's 12 ways yucky, good only to be rolled in balls and put on the hook for fish bait. I prefer a slice of pumpernickel, or seeded rye with Jewish pedigree, or a crusty French loaf, baguette, or roll. Even Pita fired over Camel droppings. Please no Wonder Bread for me

Buttered Toast Recipe

Put two slices of bread in the toaster. Adjust for lightness or darkness. Pull handle down.

Remove when the toasted bread pops up.

Smear on butter with a table knife. Jam, jelly, or peanut butter can also be smeared on the toast in lieu of butter.

Serve toast with coffee.

Simple and yummy.

I hear that toast bars are currently hot in trendy California. It figures, but maybe this time the Californians are on to something.

Grits:

stone-ground or old-fashioned grits (one cup)
heavy cream (six ounces)
unsalted butter (five-six tablespoons)
salt and fresh ground black pepper
Tabasco sauce

Boil a quart of salted water (that's four cups) in a medium pot. Slowly add a cup of grits, stirring constantly. Add a teaspoon salt and partially cover. Reduce the heat to medium and cook 15 minutes, stirring now and then. Stir in the butter and 3 tablespoons of heavy cream in the uncovered pot. Keep stirring while adding the rest of the cream, a few tablespoons at a time, until the mixture thickens and show signs of boiling. Take grits from the heat.

At the table add salt, if desired and maybe some fresh ground black pepper and a drop or two of Tabasco sauce and add more salt, if desired.

If using the grits as a base for shrimp and grits a little garlic salt stirred in doesn't hurt at all.

Fried Breakfast Potatoes:

Peel and shred six-eight good sized potatoes. Yukon Gold are good ones, but any potato will do. Slice two onions very thinly and pull apart the rings. Season potatoes and onions with salt, fresh ground black pepper, and some Cajun, Creole, or Greek seasoning mix. Fry potatoes and onions together in bacon drippings until crispy golden brown.

This is good eating.

Shrimp and Grits:

1 pound medium shrimp, peeled and deveined
6 slices of crisply fried bacon
¼ cup of flour
8 ounces sliced white mushrooms
1 bunch of green onions
3 cloves of garlic
1 cup of chicken stock (canned is okay)
Juice of a whole lemon
Tabasco sauce
Salt
Freshly ground black pepper

Cook, drain, and crumple the bacon. Reserve a tablespoon or so of the drippings in the skillet. Dredge the peeled shrimp in salt and peppered flour. Sauté the mushrooms in the reserved bacon drippings and two tablespoons of olive oil. Add the green onions and continue sautéing for a minute or two. Add the shrimp and crushed garlic and continue the sauté until shrimp are lightly browned. Stir in chicken stock, lemon juice and a few shakes of Tabasco sauce and salt and pepper to taste. Cook a few minutes more and deglaze the pan with a wooden spatula.

Using the earlier (or your own) grits recipe stir in the crumbled bacon through the grits and spoon the shrimp sauté over the grits.

Yum, yum, yummy.

Red Beans and Rice:

I often cheat and use a prepared commercial mix. Zatarain's is good. Get it in most supermarkets.

Add the sautéed trinity if you wish.

Red Beans and Rice from scratch:

One pound of red beans, picked over and rinsed.
Some bacon drippings (three-four tablespoons)
Ham hocks (one or two)
Smoked sausage (half pound)
The trinity (a cup each of chopped yellow onion,celery, green bell pepper)
Two and a half quarts of chicken stock or canned broth (or water)
Tasso or chopped ham (a third to half of a cup give or take).

Spice the redbeans

Pinch salt
a tablespoon fresh black pepper
Pinch cayenne
Three Bay leaves
Two teaspoons thyme
Some chopped parsley (optional)
Several cloves of chopped garlic
Tabasco sauce (on the table)

Cover beans with water and soak overnight. Drain and put aside. Heat bacon drippings in a large pot, add some of the Tasso or ham and cook a minute or so for flavor. Add the trinity and the first three spices and saute until soft. Now, the bay leaves, thyme, parsley, the sausage and the ham hocks (or Tasso). Cook until browned (4 or 5 minutes). Add the garlic. Now the rinsed beans and chicken broth or water.

Bring the mess to a boil, reduce heat, and simmer for about two hours. If beans get too thick add water, as needed. After two hours of simmering take the beans from the flame and remove and mash about a fourth of them with a cooking spoon. Stir in the mashed beans with the remaining three fourths of unmashed beans.

Serve red beans over boiled rice (see earlier recipe). Or mix the rice through. Your choice.

Red rice and beans goes well with fried fish or fried shrimp and, of course, cold beer.

Cajun Gruel or Dirty Rice:

1 cup long-grain rice
2 cups beef or vegetable broth, 2 cups water
3-4 Tbsp olive oil
1/2 pound ground pork
1/2 pound chicken livers chopped
1/4 pound of bacon, crisp fried and crumbled
1 yellow onion, chopped
3-4 celery stalks, chopped
1 green bell pepper
Cajun seasoning to taste
Or ½ teaspoon each of thyme, black pepper and red pepper, salt, onion powder, garlic powder to taste (I go sorta spice heavy)
Bunch of green onions, chopped

Cook the rice (per earlier recipe) but use beef or vegetable broth for one third of the cooking liquid. Let cooked rice stand for 5 minutes, coat with 1 or 2 tablespoons of olive oil.

In a large saute pan that can hold the rice plus everything else, put 1 tablespoon of oil plus the bacon and cook over medium-low heat until the bacon is crispy. Crumble. Add the ground pork and increase the heat to high to brown the meat. As the pork starts to brown, add the 1-2 tablespoons of olive oil and add the trinity (celery, green pepper, and onions). Brown them all over medium-high heat. You may notice the bottom of the pan getting crusty. Keep it from burning by lowering the heat if needed. Add saute chopped chicken liver and cook for a few minutes more.

Add the remaining beef/vegetable broth and deglaze the pan by scraping the bottom of the pan with a wooden spoon. Add the seasonings and turn the heat to high. Boil away most of the beef stock and add the cooked rice. Toss. Turn off the heat and add the green onions. Toss again and serve hot, with Tabasco sauce. Good with beer or red wine.

Crawfish or Shrimp Étouffée (means smothered):

Start with the trinity, finely diced (remember, finely diced)
Two large or three medium yellow onions
Two green bell peppers
Five/six celery stalks
Sauté in a heavy pan (preferably cast iron) using a stick of butter

Stir in spices (or a couple of tablespoons of a commercial Creole seasoning)

Add:
Several pinches kosher salt
Several pinches paprika
Half teaspoon granulated garlic
Teaspoon onion powder
Several grinds fresh ground black pepper
Pinch or two of dried thyme

Boil several pounds of crawfish tails or shrimp in vegetable stock (Swanson's works) (save about 2-3 cups of the liquid.)

Stir ¼ cup of flour into sautéed trinity add a small amount of the saved stock stirring constantly. Then add the rest of the stock to make gravy that is neither too thick nor too thin (you be the judge).

Then:
Minced garlic 4/5 tablespoons
Worcestershire sauce to taste
Tabasco sauce to taste
Green onion chopped
Parsley chopped

Add the four-five tablespoons of minced garlic, several dollops Worcestershire sauce, several shakes Tabasco sauce. Stir and simmer about 20 minutes. Toss in a bunch of chopped green onion and some chopped parsley, Stir and simmer 10 more minutes.

Then:
More butter
Lemon juice

Stir in three or four tablespoons of butter and a tablespoon of lemon juice. Taste and adjust seasonings if needed.

Add the boiled shrimp or crawfish tails and simmer for a few more minutes or until hot. Sliced Andouille sausage can be added if you desire

Serve over boiled rice. Tabasco sauce on the table.

Cold beer with this dish.

Crab cakes:

Like most of my recipes this is not precise because I use the old Redneck toss together method rather than measurements.

I pound of cooked picked crab meat, lump is best but mixed is okay

1 small onion finely diced
1 small bell pepper finely diced
1 egg (or two small) beaten with a fork or wire whisk
Half cup of rich mayonnaise
A couple of shakes of Tabasco sauce
A couple of shakes of Worcestershire sauce
Several teaspoons of Dijon Mustard
Several grinds of black pepper
A half teaspoon of garlic powder
Enough Italian flavored breadcrumbs to get the patties to hold shape while still moist

If the cakes are too dry add a bit more mayo.

Fry 'em in about an inch of very hot peanut oil. Keep flipping 'cause the breadcrumbs burn. When golden brown and hot through drain on paper towels and serve.

Serve with salad, oven roasted asparagus and red potatoes and wine or beer.

Makes for a happy tummy. Yummy.

Crab, Norfolk style:

1 lb. of cooked crab meat, butter, six-eight grinds of fresh black peppercorns, six cloves of garlic, pressed. Saute the crab in peppered garlic butter for a minute or two. Place in a ramekin, coat top with Italian flavored bread crumbs and a couple of dots of butter. Broil on high until the top is golden brown.

Twice Baked Potatoes:

Bake large baking potatoes, cut lengthwise and scoop out the pulp. Mash and mix with sour cream, salt and pepper, and some garlic and re-stuff the potato skins. Sprinkle Parmesan cheese on top and bake again until top browned lightly.

Asparagus:

1 pound of fresh asparagus. Snap off bottom stems, Roast at 400 degrees for 10 minutes or so with olive oil, garlic, salt and black pepper, red pepper flakes..

I buy crusty rolls at the bakery and Champagne at the booze store. Heat rolls in 400 degree oven, chill the Champagne.

This is our traditional Christmas eve dinner. But we eat it at other times as well. I catch the crab in our backyard tidal creek.

A word on roast vegetables:

Any root and some other veggies can be roasted with olive oil, garlic, salt and black pepper, red pepper flakes and they are delicious. Prime candidates are root vegetables including potatoes, onions, green beans, tomatoes.

Whole okra pods roasted with with boudin sausage make a great appetizer. Coat the pods lightly with garlic oil, salt and black pepper, red pepper flakes and do as above. Pam olive oil spray works well. Make sure the caps and stems stay on the okra pods to keep them from oozing and allowing them to roast properly.

Roast any veggies at 400 degrees for 10 minutes or so.

To my way of thinking roasting is the best way to cook vegetables.

Shrimp and Oyster Perloo:

Several tablespoons of extra virgin olive oil for sauteing
Country ham chopped, 1 lb.
Smoked sausage or kielbasa, 1 pound cut ¼ inch
2-3 large onions
2-3 bell peppers, chopped

Several peeled, seeded, chopped 'maters
Bunch of parsley
A bit of thyme (tsp)
Some cayenne (1/2 tsp, maybe more)
Tabasco sauce (several shakes)
Freshly ground black pepper
6 garlic cloves
Cup and a half of long grain rice
Cup of chicken broth
Three dozen oysters, shucked. Reserve the oyster liquor
Two pounds of large shrimp, peeled
Bunch of scallions, chopped

Use a big heavy pot. Heat olive oil. Saute ham and sausage till lightly browned. Add onions and peppers, spices and parsley. Cook about ten minutes, stirring now and then. Add tomatoes and garlic and cook ten more minutes, or until it thickens some. Stir in rice, chicken broth, oyster liquor. Bring to a boil and then simmer until rice is cooked. Stir in shrimp and oysters. Cover and cook about ten more minutes. Serve in shallow bowls and dress with chopped scallions.

Tabasco sauce on the table.

Cold beer. Crusty French bread. Bon appitite.

Tender, Piquant Pot Roast:

Start with a 3 and 1/2 to 4 lb. Sirloin roast
Slice a bulb of garlic (six-eight cloves)
Grind two three tbs. fresh black pepper

Using about a quarter cup of extra virgin olive oil sear the roast with the garlic and pepper. Put seared roast in a heavy pot. Roast at 400 degrees 20 minutes.

Mix together and add:
1 twelve ounce can of tomato sauce
An envelope of Lipton onion soup mix

More black pepper
Some garlic powder
A cup of medium salsa (Pace brand is good).
A little steak sauce if you have it. (obviously optional, but good)
Worcestershire sauce (several goodly dollops.)
Cut oven heat to 325 for about two hours.

Prepare:

Three lbs yellow onions (peeled and halved)
Two lbs of baby carrots
Two pounds of plum tomatoes

Quartered potatoes are an option but they'd have to be pitched in later in the process.

Put the veggies in layers atop the roast (carrots, then onions, then tomatoes). Pour two cans of V-8 (12 0z. size) over the entire mess. Keep roasting @ 325 for another hour and a half.

Delicious. The sauce is like a highly flavored beef based soup. And the recipe makes a very large smackerel, good for several meals at our place. Red wine with this one.

Chicken Marsala:

1 pound white mushrooms
2 bunches of scallions
fresh black pepper
mixed Italian seasoning (basil and oregano, fresh or dried)
2 bay leaves
Marsala wine
2 cans of Chicken broth
Flour
Olive oil
Butter

Pound and a half of skinless-boneless chicken breasts, pounded thin.

Slice mushrooms and scallions (include some scallion greens). In a large sauté pan melt a quarter pound of butter with several tablespoons of extra virgin olive oil. Sauté the mushrooms and scallions until soft.

Over medium heat add 1-quarter cup of flower stirring constantly until the flower-coated veggies are medium brown. If the flowered vegetables are too dry add olive oil while stirring. When browned add the chicken broth and a cup of Marsala wine, several grinds of black pepper, Italian seasonings and bay leaves.

Keep stirring and bring to a boil until the mixture thickens. If it's too thick add more chicken stock and Marsala wine. Remove from heat and refrigerate overnight if you can.

The overnight refrigeration isn't necessary but helps the flavor grow. When ready to cook the chicken reheat the sauce.

The Chicken:

Two chicken breasts should feed four. Pound or roll the breasts to about 1/4 to 1/3 inch thick. Cut each flattened breast in two. Salt and pepper the chicken and dredge in flour. Sauté in extra virgin olive oil for about a minute on each side of the chicken or until lightly browned. Remove to a warm platter.

Deglaze the sauté pan by pouring in a few ounces of Marsala and scraping with a wooden spoon or spatula. Pour the glace over the chicken.

Serve chicken Marsala sauce with wide boiled noodles. Ladle Marsala sauce over the plates full of chicken and pasta.

(Yankees use veal scallopini rather than chicken.
I like veal. I like chicken too.)

The Veal:

For four people sauté 1 1/2 pounds of veal scallopini. With kitchen shears snip every two inches about a half inch into the edges of the scallopini to keep from curling. Salt and pepper the scallopini and dredge with flour. Sauté in extra virgin olive oil for about a minute on each side of the scallopini or until lightly browned. Remove to a warm platter.

Deglaze the sauté pan by pouring in a few ounces of Marsala and scraping with a wooden spoon or spatula. Pour the glace over the scallopini slices.

Serve Scaloppini with wide boiled noodles. Ladle Marsala sauce over the plates full of veal and pasta.

With either chicken or veal oven roasted fresh asparagus goes well. A crusty Italian of French bread is a must. And, good red wine. Bon appetit.

Shrimp with Remolaude sauce:

Boil some large shrimp, as many as you wish.

Boiled Shrimp:

Six quarts of boiled salted water.

Add:
eight ounces of white vinegar
several goodly shakes of Tabasco sauce
Several pounds of jumbo shrimp (heads off, shells on).

Boil the shrimp for three minutes, dump in a colander, spray with cold water to stop the cooking. Drain and chill in the refrigerator.

Remolaude Sauce:

2 cups of mayonnaise
2 tablespoons Creole mustard (or any piquant mustard)
1 small grated onion
3 goodly tablespoons prepared horseradish

2 tablespoons of catchup
a little salt
Juice of one lemon
A dollop of Worcestershire sauce
Several grinds of fresh black pepper
a bit o' cayenne (quarter teaspoon)
a coupla shakes of Tabasco sauce

Mix ingredients well. Chill. Serve over cold shrimp. It's also good with cold ham or roast beef.

Shrimp, 'Mater, & Spinach Spaghetti:

Two packages of frozen chopped spinach (thawed)
Two cans of diced tomatoes
Two pounds of Jumbo shrimp (I catch 'em in the backyard creek)
6-8 cloves of pressed garlic
lots of fresh ground black pepper
a little bit of red pepper flakes
Olive oil

Sauté the garlic in olive oil and continue sauteing after adding the spinach and tomatoes. Add pepper, red pepper flakes. More oil if needed. You should end up with a saucy-oily mess. Cook the shrimp for five minutes in the sauce, stirring frequently.

Boil a pound of spaghetti (Angel Hair) al-dente. Pour shrimp, tomato, spinach mixture over spaghetti and mix thoroughly.

Serve with a crusty bread, a simple salad with vinaigrette, and a good wine. Yum!

Shrimp and Ham (or sausage) Jambalaya:

Boil white rice in salted water and set aside. The basic rice recipe will do. A cup of raw rice yields a goodly amount

Cook several pounds of shelled and deveined shrimp in boiling water for about 4-5 minutes.

In a heavy pot melt 6 tablespoons of butter. Add 1 ½ cups of finely chopped yellow onion and two tablespoons of finely chopped garlic. Cook until soft and translucent but not brown. Add a can of chopped tomatoes with liquid and three tablespoons of tomato paste.

Add a half cup of finely chopped celery and a quarter cup of finely chopped green bell pepper. Three pulverized cloves of garlic, half teaspoon of dried thyme, half teaspoon of cayenne pepper, several grinds of fresh black pepper. And a teaspoon of salt.

Stir frequently while cooking over a moderate heat until vegetables are tender and sauce thickens.

Add a pound of cubed smoked ham (smoked sausage can be substituted). Cook for five minutes. Add shrimp and then the rice and stir till liquid is absorbed.

Taste. Adjust spices with black pepper and/or Tabasco sauce.

Recipe is easily doubled, tripled, whatever.

Cajun Rice:

In a heavy pot melt 3 or 4 tablespoons of bacon drippings.

Sauté a diced onion, celery, and green bell pepper, 'bout half a cup of each.

Add crisp crumbled bacon, 'bout a quarter cup.

Add a can of diced tomato and a can of tomato sauce.

Now, 8 to 10 grinds of fresh black pepper, some red pepper flakes, some rosemary, two bay leaves and several shakes of Tabasco sauce.

Toss in a cup of white rice.

Bring the mess to a boil while stirring. Cover and cut heat to simmer for 20-25 minutes. Take from heat and let stand for 10 minutes.

Serve with smoked sausage, shrimp and/or scallops, any or all of which are good sautéed in a mix of olive oil, butter, dry white wine, black pepper, red pepper flakes, and garlic.

Serve with chilled Savignon Blanc.

Yum!

Cajun Gumbo:

First make a brown roux.
Here's how (or use the microwave method)
One cup of vegetable oil
One cup of white flour in a sifter
Some salt an' some pepper
(or half that amount for a smaller pot full)

Heat the oil real hot and sprinkle in some salt an' cracked black pepper. Now, cut the heat to medium an' slowly add the flour from the sifter while stirrin' constantly. Continue stirring until the roux turns a rich dark brown and there is a nutty smelling flavor. Remove from the heat. It takes 'bout a half hour of constant stirrin' to be sure that the roux doesn't burn. Remember rule1: Throw the roux out an start again if it does burn.

Chop up the Cajun trinity, a couple of large yellow onions, three-four green bell peppers, an' a bunch of celery. Throw the veg in the roux an sauté carefully. Add about a pound and a half of sliced okra to the sauté.

When the veg is cooked through add two or tree quarts of chicken or fish stock, whichever you prefer, an' start heating. (the fish stock can be made from boiling shrimp heads an' shells in water with some busted up carrots and celery, an' green onions and adding some spice to the boil. For chicken broth I cheat an' use the canned stuff. Bar Harbor canned fish stock also works well.)

Add some chopped up tomatoes, maybe six small one or three or four medium. (Strictly speakin', 'maters make the gumbo into a Creole rather than a Cajun dish, but so what?)

Spice the whole mess up with a teaspoon of red pepper flakes and several shakes of Tabasco sauce. Add more cracked black pepper and a couple of bay leaves.

Bring the mess to a boil an then simmer for a couple of hours while having a couple of cold ones.

About an hour before serving cut up some andouille sausage and some chicken or duck meat an' add it to the simmer. If the gumbo need thickening you can use some salt and peppered flour dissolved in some of the stock. Or some filé powder for thickening if Okra is not in season and the Gumbo is too thin.

Last thing to do is add the seafood, shrimp, oysters, and cooked blue crab meat. Let that final mess simmer fifteen-twenty minutes.

Note: The Gumbo can be sausage and duck or chicken, or sausage an' seafood, or it can be all of that stuff thrown together.

It's your choice.

Serve the gumbo over boiled long-grain white rice and with what ever cold long-necks you didn't drink during the cooking. A crusty baguette goes good as well.

Meatloaf:

Three-three and a half pounds of good ground beef. Try using ground chuck with maybe a pound or so of ground round Three quarters of a pound of ground pork, and three quarters of a pound of ground veal. If you don't have veal use a half teaspoon of Knox gelatin, that works.

Mix up:

Two eggs.
Half cup of catchup (use Heinz if you can).
Two teaspoon soy sauce
Two tablespoons of Worcestershire sauce
Several goodly shakes of Tabaso ®
Half a teaspoon of Knox unflavored gelatin. *

On top the meat dump 2/3 cup of crumbled saltines (or Italian style bread crumbs), one finely chopped onion. six garlic cloves minced fine, oregano and basil to taste. Lots of fresh ground black pepper. Some salt.

Throw in the egg, gelatin and condiment mixture.

Knead the meatloaf till all of the stuff is mixed in well. Make into a loaf. Put a rack in a roast pan so the fat can drain away. Cook for an hour and ten minutes or if you have a meat thermometer until the loaf is 140-150 degree F.

That's all. It's good eatin'.

----

*The secret to a yummy meatloaf is either veal or unflavored Knox gelatin. That's right, you heard correctly. A half teaspoon of gelatin to three-three and a half pounds of ground beef mixed with three quarters of a pound of ground pork mimics about a pound of ground veal for keeping the meatloaf nice and moist. And unlike the veal gelatin hardly costs anything.

Burgers:

Here's a good way to make the burgers. A pound and a half of good burger meat --ground round/chuck mixed is the best. A half teaspoon of Knox unflavored gelatin. Dice up an onion real fine. Add the onion to the meat with some catchup, and Worcestershire sauce and an some Tabasco sauce. Spice the mix wit a little salt, a lots of fresh ground black pepper. Toss in some mixed Italian herbs. Mix it all together and it'll be a runny mess at this point. Add just enough dry bread crumbs or cracker crumbs to firm up the mess. Shape into four big patties. Refrigerate to firm up some more.

Broil on the charcoal or gas grill. Serve on a toasted bun wit more catchup and a slice of onion. If you only need two pattys freeze the others.

Cuke, Tomato, Onion Salad (goes good with burgers):

Two ripe tomatoes, diced in largish pieces
A large onion diced the same
Two peeled cucumbers also diced
Lots of freshly ground pepper

Greek vinaigrette dressing, several ounces (Farmer Boy brand is good).

Mix thoroughly and refrigerate

Variations:

Crumble in some feta cheese

Add some kalmata olives

A substitute dressing is red wine vinegar and extra virgin olive oil with garlic and herbs.

Roasted Peppers:

Paper Bag Method

Six red bell peppers. Wash and dry the peppers. Set broiler on medium and set the rack 6 inches from the flame or electric coil. Roast, turning frequently to prevent burning, for about 10 minutes (until the skin blisters and blackens on all sides).

Remove peppers and put them in a tightly closed brown paper bag. Let stand for ten minutes. This process will make removing the skins easy.

Remove skins and seeds.

Cut the peppers into 1/2 to 3/4 inch strips. Mix a couple of tablespoons of olive oil with oregano, salt, minced garlic and crushed red pepper seeds. Marinate the peppers in this stuff.

Great with meat dishes, with an antipasto, or on sandwiches (Po-boys or Italian Hoagies) or on burgers. You can also toss them into the spaghetti sauce.

Baked Beans:

This is a recipe for doctoring up canned beans. I always start with Bush's Original baked beans. Use your own favorites.

6-8 cans of beans
In a big mixing bowl add as much as you like, I'm fairly generous:
Brown sugar, 2/3 cup
Finely diced onion (fresh or dried)
Yellow mustard
Catsup
Worchester sauce
Tabasco saucc
A1 Sauce
Freshly ground black pepper
Sea salt
Garlic powder

Mix well. Pour into a large Pyrex baking dish and layer with strips of quality bacon. Bake at 325 for about two hours, ckecking occasionally.

Macaroni Salad:
Cook one pound of elbow macaroni –al dente
Dice 4-6 celery stalks finely
Add about a cup of real mayonaise (sometimes with a little olive oil).
Freshly ground black pepper
Some salt
Some celery salt
Mix well and chill in the refrigerator. Add more Mayo if needed.

Potato Salad:

I make it the same way as the macaroni salad, but using boiled redskin potatos. Sometimes I add a little shaved onion and green pepper.

The beans and the salads are simple but yummy. Try 'em with burgers, or steaks, or pulled pork or fried chicken or fried fish or shrimp.

Stuffed Mushroom Appetizers:

12 to 18 large white mushrooms caps. Remove stems and chop them finely.
One onion finely chopped
A half cup of cashews or pistachios finely chopped
A half cup of sun dried tomatoes in olive oil finely chopped
Several cloves of garlic finely chopped
Fresh ground black pepper.
Sausage meat

Sauté all of the sausage and chopped stuff over medium heat for a few minutes. Stuff the mushroom caps with the concoction. Sprinkle grated Parmesan cheese over the stuffed mushrooms.

Bake at 350 for 10-15 minutes or until the mushrooms are done to your taste. Yummy.

This recipe is from my son-in-law, Bob Parfitt.

Rainy Day Chile:

Sauté three pounds of good quality ground beef in a heavy pot. Drain drippings.

Add:

Two large cans of red kidney beans with juice
Two medium cans of black beans with juice

Two medium cans of white beans (Cannolini or Great Northern)
Two medium cans of Italian tomatoes (drained)
A cup of diced onions
Four or Five tablespoons of chili powder
(a mixture of ground chili pepper, cumin, salt, oregano, and garlic)
A couple of spoonfuls of cumin
A healthy grinding of fresh black pepper
(I salt to taste at the table)
Three four ounces of red wine vinegar. Swish the vinegar from bean can to bean can to get out all of the good thickening starches.

Stir everything together and bring to a boil while stirring. Simmer on very low heat for about two hours or longer

It's good served as is or dressed with shredded cheese and diced raw onions. If a spicier dish is desired more chili powder or cumin and Tabasco sauce can be stirred in at the table. Accompany with saltine crackers

Variations:

Serve over cooked spaghetti (Chili Mac) or boiled rice.
Slop it over a baked potato.

Beer is a necessary accoutrement to any chili. You just have to have it. Enjoy.

Frogmore Stew:

Best made outdoors in huge quantities. Here's the indoor recipe.

Get a big stainless steel or enamel cook pot, 16 quart. Fill half way with water. Dump in about 3/4 cup of Old Bay seasoning (or any shellfish boil seasoning) and a pound of butter. Bring to boil.

Add a bunch (5-7 lbs.) of redskin potatoes quartered and three lbs. of yellow onions quartered. Add three pounds of sliced smoked sausage (Hillshire Farms Brand is good, but there are many others). Let this stuff come back to a boil.

Add six ears of sweet corn (broken in halves). Bring back to a boil again.

Add five pounds of shrimp (in the shell) and reboil.

Pour off liquid and serve in big soup bowls.

Top each bowl with two or three steamed blue crabs.

Cold beer is a must have with Frogmore stew.

Serves a whole bunch of people or a few piggy types.

Bon Appetit. Burp!!!

Basic Creole Sauce:

Looking for some good eating. If you have some shrimp. Or some fish. Or scallops. Or mussels. Or any combination of this stuff. Here's is what you want to do.

In a heavy pot:

Fry 1 lb of bacon until crisp, remove bacon.

Sauté 3 lbs of strong sliced yellow onions and a couple of sliced green bell peppers in the bacon drippings until the stuff is limp and the onions are opaque.

Add to the peppers/onions mix:

Three cans of diced tomatoes
Two small cans of tomato paste

One 12 oz. can of V-8 juice (or tomato juice).

Stir around some and add:

Several tablespoons of fresh ground black pepper
6-8 cloves of pressed garlic
Many shakes of Worcestershire sauce
Several shakes of Tabasco Sauce
Some salt (not much)
1 short tablespoon of granulated sugar

Crumble the crisp bacon and toss that in the pot.

Bring the whole mess to a boil while stirring. Cover, simmer for several hours. This stuff grows with time so it's best if reheated and served the next day. When very hot add several pounds of peeled shrimp or firm white fish, or scallops, or mussels, or all of that stuff and cook until done. About five minutes.

Serve over boiled white rice. A crusty loaf of bread and a chilled Savignon Blanc goes good.

I love this stuff. Yeah man, I truly do. So will you.

Spaghetti (my way):

3 pounds of ground chuck

I cheat and start with 6 to 8 fifteen oz. cans of Hunts basic tomato sauce. You'll need to add:

1 large tablespoon of garlic powder or 6-8 crushed cloves of fresh garlic
1 large tablespoon of freshly ground black pepper.

A small handful of mixed Italian herbs
Three bay leaves
Some extra virgin olive oil

Sauté the chuck until brown. Use a little olive oil for flavor. Drain liquid. Add the the cans of basic tomato sauce, garlic, freshly ground black pepper, mixed Italian herbs. Rub the herbs between your thumb and forefinger to release aromatic oils.

Add a dollop of extra virgin olive oil.

Simmer on very low heat for several hours.

Bring three-four quarts of salted water to a boil and cook a pound of spaghetti *al-dente* (about nine minutes). Pour half of the sauce over the spaghetti, stir and serve. Freeze the remaining sauce.

Goes well with garlic bread and dry red wine. Slurping good. And cheap.

Heart Busting Beef Burgundy:

1 pound bacon
3 pounds of good stew beef
3 medium onions
1 half pound of carrot strips
1 pound white mushrooms (medium size)
1 quarter cup of olive oil
2 twelve ounce cans of beef broth
2 cups of decent red wine
1 tablespoon of tomato paste
1/2 teaspoon thyme, 2 bay leaves,10-12 grinds of fresh black pepper
1/4 pound of butter (one stick)

In a heavy pot fry a pound of sliced bacon in olive oil until crisp, Remove bacon, drain over paper towels and crumble. In the olive oil bacon drippings mixture sauté 3 pounds of 1 ½ inch squares of high quality stew beef. If at all fatty or gristly trim. Brown the meat on all sides using tongs (not a fork) to turn. The beef should be dark brown on all sides. Remove beef and drain fat. Pour off most of the oil/bacon drippings so that only three or four tablespoons remain. Sauté three medium sized onions and a half pound of carrot strips with 4 or 5 cloves of chopped garlic in the remaining oil/bacon dripping mixture. Sauté until onions are soft and brown. Stir in 4 tablespoons of all purpose flour into the sautéed veggies. Return crumbled bacon and browned beef cubes to the pot.

Stir in:

2 cans of beef broth

2 cups of a good (palatable) red wine. Merlot, Cabernet Savignon, or whatever full bodied wine you prefer.

1 tablespoon of tomato paste

½ teaspoon thyme

2 bay leafs.

10-12 grinds of fresh black pepper.

Bring to a boil, cut back to simmer for two, two and a half hours or until beef is tender. Remove beef and veggies and reduce sauce until it thickens. If it gets too thick just thin out with more beef broth or wine. Meanwhile sauté 1 pound of medium whole white mushrooms in a quarter pound of butter until soft. Toss 'em and the butter in with the beef/veggies. Put the whole mess in the burgundy gravy.

Refrigerate overnight. The flavor will grow. The next day just cook wide egg noodles and reheat the beef burgundy over a low flame.

Serve over noodles with a good, crusty French bread and red wine of your choice.

Mmmmmmm! Good!

Shrimo Diablo:

In a large sauté pan:

¼ cup of good quality olive oil
½ cup of good red wine (I used cabernet sauvignon)
1 can diced tomatoes
1 small can of tomato paste
six ounces of sun dry tomatoes
six-eight cloves of pressed garlic
½ teaspoon red pepper flakes
several shakes of Tabasco sauce
several grinds of fresh black pepper
a touch of sea salt

Bring to a boil while stirring and then simmer for an hour or so. Right before serving boil a pound of angel hair pasta and toss the shrimp into the sauce and cook for about five minutes over medium high heat. Toss the sauced shrimp and pasta together and serve.

I serve this with a green salad with red wine vinegar/oil dressing and a crusty French bread. Some nice wine.

It's yum.

Supper Shrimp:

I caught a couple of pounds of nice big shrimp so supper is sautéed shrimp with angel hair pasta. You can get your shrimp at the market.

2 pounds of headed, shelled shrimp. I like the big ones.
1 half cup of extra virgin olive oil
3 tablespoons of tomato paste
1 can of diced tomatoes
1 cup of sun dried tomatoes
2-3 tablespoons of freshly ground black pepper
10-12 cloves of finely chopped garlic

Use your judgment for:

Some oregano
Some basil
Some chopped parsley

1 pound of angel hair pasta boiled in salted water per instructions on the package.

In a large sauté pan combine all of the ingredients except the shrimp and pasta. Sauté over medium high heat for ten-fifteen minutes stirring frequently. Then boil the pasta for about five minutes. Stir the shrimp into the sauce at high heat for three to five minutes. Drain the pasta and stir it into the sauce/shrimp mixture.

Serve hot with a crusty baguette and a nice red wine. That's supper. *Mmmmmmm*, yes!

Fried Shrimp:

Cook as much or as little as you want. I think a pound is minimum. Of course, I catch them in the backyard tidal creek. You may have to get them at the market.

1 pound of extra jumbo (oxymoronic) shrimp (about 18 per pound), headed, peeled, devined. Smaller shrimp can be used. I sometimes do.

Egg wash:

Two-three eggs whipped with salt, pepper, red pepper flakes (and to taste Cajun or Creole seasoning). Maybe a drop or two of Tabasco sauce.

Breading:

I use commercial breading, Zaterain's or House Autry. Saltines rolled with your mama's wooden or marble rolling pin will work, or they can be crushed in a blender. Or, a spiced up cornmeal-white flour mix makes a fine coating (breading) material.

Drop the shrimp in a bowl filled with the egg wash. Put the breading in a plastic bag and with tongs add the egg washed shrimp. Shake well.

In a large frying or sauté pan put in about a half to three quarters of a inch of canola or peanut oil. Heat to near the smoke point. Cook the shrimp in batches for about three minutes. Drain on paper towels.

Serve the shrimp with lemon, or cocktail sauce, or Remolaude sauce (see earlier recipe).

Fried shrimp is good with red beans and rice and a salad, or perhaps just a salad. A nice wine (white) or a cold beer goes well.

Who-weee, good!

Pan Seared Sea Scallops:

1 pound of sea scallops (12 to 15)
butter and olive oil
fresh ground peppercorns
red pepper flakes
Creole seasoning (optional)

Mix together several tablespoons each of butter and olive oil. Stir in pepper, red pepper flakes to taste. Add Creole seasoning if desired.

On the kitchen range heat a large cast iron frying pan until very hot. Coat the pan thinly with the butter-olive oil mixture. It will get near to the smoke point almost immediately.

Add the sea scallops. Turn frequently with tongs.

The scallops will cook to a crusty golden or slightly darker brown. The trick is to keep an eye on the scallops as they cook and turn frequently enough to prevent burning.

I like to serve this with oven roasted redskin potatoes and oven roasted asparagus. A Greek or Caesar salad goes well. Of course, a nice white wine or a quality cold beer.

Bon Appetit.

Pasta Fazoole:

Sauté in a large, heavy pot 2 pounds of good quality stew beef in 1-1 1/2 inch cubes with three tablespoons of good quality olive oil until brown. I sometimes use sirloin but if you do bigger pieces are needed as it's very tender stuff. I have a Lodge cast iron pot, which is great but not absolutely necessary. Recipe is easily doubled or tripled.

Add:

two-three chopped onions (big ones)
cup or more of chopped celery
cup or more shredded carrots

Continuing sautéing for about 10-15 minutes over low heat. Add olive oil if needed.

Add:

1 can of diced tomatoes
1 can of stewed tomatoes
1 can of red kidney beans
1 can of white kidney beans (cannelloni)
(do not drain the tomatoes or beans)
three cans of beef broth
1 can of plain tomato sauce
1 12 oz can of V-8 juice, maybe two
6 to 8 ounces of good red wine (plus 4 for the cook), I like Cabernet Savignon.
8-10 grinds of black pepper
oregano to taste
a bunch of chopped parsley
two bay leafs
Several goodly shakes of Tabasco sauce (fear not)
Six-eight cloves of garlic, pressed

Simmer the soup for two hours or more and then let sit all afternoon. Bring back to boil, add a half pound of pasta (I use small shells) Cook another half hour.

Serve with crusty French bread, an Italian salad, and red wine. Yummy!

Mimi's Chicken and Egg Plant in Red Sauce:

Prepare red sauce a day or two ahead.

6 cans of Hunt's tomato sauce
2 cans of diced tomatoes
12-15 grinds of fresh black pepper
2 tsp of garlic powder or 8 cloves crushed
some red pepper flakcs (not too many, maybe 12 to 20)
2-3 tbs Italian herbs (squeeze between thumb and forefinger to release oils.
3 bay leaves

Bring to a boil while stirring, cut heat and simmer two-three hours. Put in a glass bowl, cover, and refrigerate for a day or two.

Now the goodies:

6-8 Skinless, boneless chicken breasts
3 firm eggplants (Aubergines)
12-16 slices of mozzarella cheese

Whip up four eggs and put in a shallow dish. Mix a bunch of Italian flavored bread crumbs, black pepper, garlic powder or granules, and grated Parmesan cheese. Spread over a platter.

Dredge 6-8 skinless-boneless chicken breasts in egg then bread crumb mixture. Set aside.

Peel and slice lengthwise (about 1/2 inch thick) 3 firm eggplants. Pile slices on a plate or waxed paper, place a plate on top of the slices and put a heavy weight on it. This presses any bitter liquid from the eggplant slices.

In a heavy sauté pan fry the chicken breasts in olive oil turning until a golden brown.

Now, dredge the eggplant slices in the egg breadcrumb mixture. Fry the eggplant the same as the chicken breasts.

Now, get a large shallow Pyrex (or other oven wear) dish or two. Pour some red sauce in the bottom. Place the chicken breasts.

A slice of mozzarella on each breast, more red sauce

A slice of eggplant atop each breast and cheese pile.

A slice of mozzarella on each pile

More red sauce

Bake the piles for 45 minutes at 350 degrees. Heat the extra sauce.

Serve on plates with extra red sauce drizzled on. Good with spaghetti or wide egg noodles and crusty French bread or rolls and a salad with oil/vinegar dressing. Don't forget the red wine.

Bon appetit.

Portabella Mushroom with Italian Sausage Concoction:

If you like Italian food here's a taste treat.

4 large portabella mushroom caps

1 lb. bulk Italian sausage (I use Jimmy Dean brand)
8 slices of mozzarella cheese
1 can or bottle of roasted red bell peppers
1 can of hunts tomato sauce
8-10 garlic cloves (pressed)
lots of fresh ground black pepper

4 tablespoons extra virgin olive oil (I know, I know. Who cares what the olives do.)

Scramble the sausage over medium heat. Place mushrooms cap side down in a Pyrex or other ovenproof dish. Mix the olive oil, some black pepper, and some pressed garlic and drizzle over the mushrooms.

Put a good sized piece of roasted red bell pepper atop each mushroom. Put two slices of mozzarella cheese atop each mushroom. Top the cheese with the Italian sausage

Add black pepper and the remaining crushed garlic to the tomato sauce, heating and stirring thoroughly. Pour sauce over the sausage/cheese/mushrooms and bake at 325 degrees for about a half hour.

Serve with a green salad, a crusty bread, and a good red wine.

It's good. Enjoy

Fried Fish:

Sac-a-lait:

If you're not from Bayou country the fish are also called white perch or crappie (that's pronounced like the farmer's crop).

Fillet the fish. Shake some salt and black pepper, and some cayenne pepper on the fillets. Coat the fish fillets with yellow mustard.

Put the fillets in a big plastic or paper bag with fish fry mix (a mix of fine ground corn meal and corn flour with spices and shake to coat them. We buy fry mix at the market in big sacks.

Put about three quarters of an inch of peanut oil in a large frying pan and get it real hot. Fry fry the fish until they are golden brown and crispy. Drain on paper towels.

Fried Fish another way:

Use any whitefish fillet, Flounder, talipia, etc. Dip in an egg wash and coat with a commercial fish fry mix. There's no mustard in the coating.

Fry the fish in very hot peanut oil as above.

Serve the fish with lemon wedges and a Remoulade sauce (see recipe, earlier). Cole slaw is nice. Maybe some corn on the cob with butter. And, of course, cold beer. That's good eating.

Egg Wash

Here's a little recipe for an egg wash that's good for fried fish, fried shrimp, and fried veggies like okra, green beans, or asparagus.

Whip two eggs with a fork

Add:

Several grinds of fresh black pepper
A little sea salt
Some red pepper flakes
Garlic powder or creole seasoning (your taste)

Whip it all together. Coat the stuff to be fried and drop it into a plastic bag with a breading mixture. I like commercial breading mixes from the supermarket, especially Zatarain's mix.

Fred's Special Grits with Fish: *

Yellow (stone ground) grits or Bob's Red Mill grits 1 cup
Cherry tomatos, a dozen or so
Sweet onion, medium

Sharp cheddar cheese ¼ cup or half a handful
Colby Jack cheese ¼ cup or half a handful
Butter several pats or tablespoons
Salt
Black pepper (preferably fresh ground)

Cook the grits as directed on the package.

Sauté cherry tomatos and sliced onion in butter with some salt and black pepper. Shred the cheddar and colby cheeses and add to the sauteed mixture with some butter and a little extra salt and pepper. Mix together with the grits.

Fry the fish fillets (see fried fish recipe above) pull the meat apart and and stir fish pieces through the grits mixture or ladle the grits over the whole fish fillets.

Shrimp can be substituted. This is yummy good stuff, especially with a cold beer.

* Recipe provided by Francis O'Brien and credited to his Father-in-Law Fridrik Tiedemann.

Fried Chicken:

2-3 eggs
1/3 cup water
teaspoon or two of Tabasco sauce
2 cups self-rising flour
several grinds of fresh black black pepper
1 plump chicken, cut into pieces
Oil, for frying, preferably peanut oil

In a medium size bowl, beat the eggs with the water. Add Tabasco sauce to taste.

In another bowl, combine the flour and pepper.

Season the chicken with salt, pepper, and garlic powder mixed.

Dip the seasoned chicken in the egg, and then coat well in the flour mixture.

In a deep pot heat the oil to 350 degrees F. Don't fill the
pot too high with oil.

Fry the chicken til brown and crisp. Maybe 12-15 minutes.

It is good. Especially with greens, mashed potatoes, and buttered corn on the cob. Oh yeah, cold beer.

Roast Chicken:

1 six pound roasting chicken
Salt and Pepper
Kitchen Bouquet

Take the chicken from the refrigerator and bring to room temperature. Remove giblets, neck, and pop up timer (if there is one). Heart, liver, and giblets can be cooked, chopped, and later added to gravy if desired.

Salt and pepper the chicken inside and out. Coat the chicken's skin with Kitchen Bouquet. Roast at 425 degrees for an hour and a half and until skin is a deep brown. Insert an instant read thermometer in the breast. It should read 180 degrees.

Remove from heat and let stand fifteen minutes before carving and serving.

Make a Gravy:

I put a bunch of ice cubes for a few minutes into the pan drippings to congeal and skim off the fat. Remove the cubes that remain.

Then with a wooden spatula and some chicken broth if needed I deglaze the pan. Now, mix flour, salt, pepper and some garlic powder with chicken broth. Put the stuff in a cocktail shaker and shake well until smooth. The flour-broth mixture goes into the cooled roast chicken drippings. Bring to a boil while stirring. Add some Kitchen Bouquet to brown up the gravy.

Continue to boil and stir until gravy thickens. If too thick add some chicken broth.

Carve the chicken and serve with garlic mashed potatoes (skins not removed) and a vegetable or vegetables of choice. Slather on the gravy.

There's not a thing in the world wrong with Stove Top stuffing.

Enjoy.

Country-fried Steak:

A pound and a half or two pounds of cube steaks
Ground pepper (from fresh peppercorns)
Salt
Canola or peanut oil
All-purpose flour
Onions

Put cube steak pieces between sheets of wax paper and with a meat tenderizer or rolling pin, gently pound the meat to tenderize it. Season piece of steak with salt and pepper.

Mix a cup and a half of flour with salt and pepper in large bowl or a plastic zip-lock bag.

Use a big sauté pan or cast-iron skillet, fill with canola oil about 1/4-inch deep. Warm over medium-high heat. While the oil is heating, dredge cube steak pieces in the seasoned flour or drop them into the zip-lock bag with the flour concoction and shake to coat well.

Cook the steak pieces in the heated oil in batches (do not overcrowd). Raise the heat a bit and cook until golden, about 3 to 4 minutes per side. Remove, transfer to a crock-pot set to warm.

The onions:

Sauté a bunch of thinly sliced onions in the pan drippings until limp and near transparent. Heap on top of the steaks in the crock-pot.

The brown gravy:

2 tablespoons reserved oil from the fried cube steaks and onions, or use bacon fat
One and a half or two tablespoons of flour
One half cup whole milk
One and a half cups chicken or beef stock
Ground ground pepper
Salt

Remove all but 2 tablespoons of oil from the sauté pan. Warm over medium-high heat and deglaze the pan by scraping. Add one and a half tablespoons (or a little more) flour to the scrapings and whisk to create a roux. Add the milk and beef or chicken stock, whisking to incorporate it with roux until gravy comes to a boil. Reduce heat to low, letting gravy cook and thicken to desire consistency, about 8 to 10 minutes. Season with salt and pepper.

Pour the gravy in the crock-pot and simmer for an hour or two.

Goes good with boiled rice. Maybe some green beans, butter beans, or corn, or all three.

Yum!

A lot of credit goes to my good cookin' buddy Kevin Livingston who helped me with this one. More than a few times I've died and gone to heaven with Kevin's country steak.

Chicken Fried Steak with White Gravy:

Use the country steak recipe but substitute self- rising flour for all purpose flour. Also make a seasoned milk mixture with a cup and a half of whole milk, two beaten eggs, salt, pepper, and Cajun seasoning. Dredge steaks in self-rising flour, dredge in the milk/egg wash, dredge in flour again. Fry until golden brown and crispy. No onions.

White Gravy:

Add butter to the pan drippings to equal about a quarter cup of fat. Sprinkle in 1/4 cup of seasoned flour, and cook and stir constantly. Scrape all the browned bits from the bottom of the pan. Cook until mixture is blended in and a very light blond color. Whisk in a cup and a half of whole milk, boil, reduce heat and stir constantly while cooking and it begins to thicken Adjust with more milk if and as needed. Season with salt and freshly ground black pepper and Cajun seasoning. Ladle over the chicken fried steaks.

Either country steak or Chicken fried steak are good eating. Try 'em both. Enjoy 'em both.

Mashed Potatoes:

Three/four pounds of redskin potatoes

Whole milk
Butter
Salt and Pepper
Six cloves of garlic (optional)

Slice redskin potatoes in half (quarters for big ones) and boil in salted water until fork tender. Run potatoes (skins and all) through a ricer into a big mixing bowl. (A simple potato masher will do if you don't have a ricer.) Add a little whole milk some butter, salt and pepper and (if you want) crushed garlic, Finish with a wire whisk for best results, making sure to use just enough milk to give the potatoes a smooth texture.

Mashed potatoes are a must with any meat (roasted beef, turkey, pork, chicken, etc) that's served with a savory gravy.

Yum, yum, yum.

Tater Cakes:

Left over mashed potatoes can be mixed with a little salted and peppered all purpose flour, formed into patties and fried in butter or a butter-bacon dripping mixture until golden brown and slightly crusty. They are delicious done this way. Add some onion and/or garlic.

Collard Greens:

a bunch of collards
a can of chicken or vegetable stock and a can water

Meat for the greens:

cooked ham,
or Tasso
or cooked sausage

or a pork chop or two
add some bacon, with drippings
or some fatback.

Wash and stack greens on top of each other. Cut across greens to make one-inch strips.

In large pot add stock, water, and the greens meat. Bring to boil, add meat and cover and reduce heat to a gentle simmer. The greens should simmer about two and a half hours. Stir pot every half-hour and add water if necessary. Recipe is easily doubled or tripled. A vinegar pepper sauce completes the dish.

Bon appetit!

Butter Beans:

Baby Lima (butter) beans, fresh in the shell
(or a package of shelled green butter beans frozen).
a little salt.
2-3 tablespoons butter
several grinds of fresh black pepper

Shell the beans if necessary and wash thoroughly. Put 2 cups water and the salt in a medium saucepan and add the beans. Cook about 30 minutes. They should be tender.

Drain the liquid and add the butter. Grind black pepper to taste before serving.

Corn On The Cob:

Shuck and boil the corn for twenty-twenty five minutes. Butter and salt and pepper. And enjoy. Or cook it in the microwave.

Microwaved Corn On The Cob:

Leave corn in the husk.

Microwave on high for 2 to 2.5 minutes per ear.

Remove from microwave. While wearing a heat proof glove cut the butt end of the ear of corn off. Hold by the top and shake. The ear of corn will slide from the husk leaving all of or most of the silk behind. Remove the few silk stragglers and butter, salt and pepper and enjoy.

This is a simple but excellent way of cooking corn on the cob.

All of these veggie sides are special good, especially with hearty meat dishes.

Yum!

Corn Bread:

I always cheat and get a good cornbread mix at the Supermarket. Bake it in a lightly greased cast iron skillet.

Bread Pudding:

Loaf of stale French bread
cup of heavy cream
6-8 eggs
6 cups of whole milk
4 cups of sugar
1/2 tsp. nutmeg, ground
4 tbs. cinnamon, ground
1/4 cup of vanilla extract
two sticks of unsalted butter
Half cup of raisins

Break bread into small pieces. Simmer milk, cream and butter until butter is melted. Add milk to the bread and mix until absorbed. Whip eggs until combined. Add eggs and the sugar, cinnamon, nutmeg and vanilla extract to bread and mix and all of the bread is softened.

In a 12x10x2 1/2 inch pan (sprinkle raisins on top) bake at 350 degrees until top is brown and middle is done, About 1 and a 1/2 hours.

Sauce:

Two sticks of unsalted Butter
1/2 cup of brown sugar
1/4 tsp. cinnamon
pinch of nutmeg
2 oz. good brandy

Mix all ingredients except and simmer for a few minutes. Cream the butter and stir into the simmered mixture until it is all blended. Pour over bread pudding.

Banana Pudding:

Take three eggs and beat in a cup of sugar. Add a pinch of salt, two cups of milk and two tablespoons of cornstarch. Boil, cut heat to medium while stirring constantly until thickened. Remove from heat and stir in a teaspoon of vanilla extract. Slice 4 ripe bananas. Layer bananas and pudding in a large Pyrex baking-serving dish. Layer the top with Nilla® wafers.

This stuff is good, especially as dessert to a pulled pork supper.

Sautéed Calf's Liver:

One of my favorites. Not my wife's favorite. I belong to a liver club. We cook liver and drink wine when the ladies are elsewhere. That way we stay in their good graces.

1 pound of thinly sliced calf's liver
Good quality olive oil
1 to 1 and ½ cup of all purpose flour
Fresh ground black pepper
Salt

Mix the flour with salt and freshly ground black pepper and put it in a shallow dish. Dredge liver in the flour mixture.

In a large sauté pan with olive oil sauté liver slices for about a minute, turn and cook a minute more. Remove liver from pan, platter, and place in a warm (170 degree) oven.

Deglaze the pan with a red wine and a wooden spatula. If more flour is needed, stir it in. Add some canned beef broth and a good quality red wine. Spice with salt, pepper, and some garlic powder. Bring to a boil while stirring and allow the gravy to thicken. If the mixture is too thick use a little more wine and/or beef stock.

Serve the sautéed calf's liver with boiled rice. Slather gravy over the calf's liver and rice. I like butter beans as the go with vegetable, but many other vegetables will do. If you are wise you've saved some of the red wine to serve with this treat.

Bon Appetit.

Fried Turkey:

Turkey fried in oil outdoors is the absolute best way to cook the bird. Do it right (which is not difficult) and it will be juicy and delicious.

You'll need a turkey frying apparatus.

Propane burner
Tank of propane
Large pot, with a strainer basket insert
Long probe thermometer
A flat outdoor surface away from things that could catch fire (Houses, garages, decks, cars and trucks, etc,)
A garden hose for cleaning tables, thawing frozen propane (rare, but it happens) and other contingencies and cleanups is a good idea.

Note: You can get the complete turkey fryer outfit (burner, pot, basket, thermometer, etc.) at any of the large chain stores (Lowe's, Home Depot, Sam's Costco, Target, Wal-Mart, etc.) They come in different sizes. We have a single turkey pot and a three at a time huge pot available through friends and neighbors. Sharing the cost of apparatus with others makes sense.

Ten pound turkey(s)

At least 5 gallons of high temp cooking oil, depending on how many turkeys. I prefer peanut but others will do fine.

Seasoning. I use Tony Cachares Creole seasoning.®

To figure out how much oil is needed put a ten pound turkey in the pot and cover with water. Mark the pot and that's the oil level (never more than three quarters full). Dry pot. Fill to line and heat the oil to 350 degrees.

Wash and dry the turkey(s) inside and out. You won't need the neck or giblet package unless you want them for another recipe. Now rub the bird(s) inside and out with the Creole seasoning. Use plenty.

Put the turkey(s) in the strainer basket and lower carefully into the hot oil. We use two men with a broom handle under the basket's bail (handle). Lower very slowly and carefully as the oil will bubble up in a roiling boil. Cook for three minutes a pound and an extra five minutes per bird. That's 35 minutes for a ten pounder.

Remove turkey, wrap in tinfoil, and let rest in a container (like a large Igloo or Yeti cooler) for a half hour or so.

Carve and Enjoy. Succulent!

I learned turkey frying from my good friend Johnny Harvey. His turkeys always come out perfect.

Making good smooth, greaseless gravies:

Two methods: Gravy from roasts and pan drippings gravy.

From Roasts:

From a roast, chicken, turkey, beef, or pork. Let the pan drippings cool until fat congeals. Skim the fat off so that only stock remains. If you don't have time to let the stuff cool stir in a bunch of ice cubes and ladle them out with fat stuck to them.

For beef gravy use beef broth as the liquid. For chicken, turkey, or pork use chicken broth..

Mix several tablespoons of all purpose flour with a can the broth until it is smooth. I use a cocktail shaker. Pour into the cooled stock from the roast. Cool is the secret to no lumps. Stir over medium heat until it begins to boil and thicken. Pour in more broth and continue stirring. Keep adding broth until it gets to the right consistency. If the gravy becomes too thin add more broth/flour mixture. I spice my gravy with fresh ground black pepper and herbs –a basil, rosemary, thyme mixture.

From Sauté Pan Drippings:

Scrape up the drippings while deglazing the pan with broth or wine. Stir in some flour and cook to a roux (light to medium brown) over medium heat. Stir the roux constantly and adjust the flame as needed to make sure it does not burn. When roux is ready proceed as in the above recipe, adding a little broth at a time while stirring to achieve the right consistency.

Adding wine or a little tomato paste helps some gravies. You be the judge.

Fried green tomatoes. Two Styles:

Basic:

Slice green tomatoes about a quarter inch thick. Fry them in bacon drippings. Make sure there's enough fat in the pan to near cover them. When they get a brown edge and are cooked through drain in paper towels. Salt and pepper 'em and eat 'em.

Advanced:

Whip up a couple of eggs with salt, pepper, garlic powder and drag quarter inch green tomato slices through it. Dredge the slices in a prepared fish or chicken batter (I like Zaterains) or a mixture of fine corn meal and white flower. Deep fry the green tomato slices in very hot peanut oil until golden brown. Drain on paper towels and serve with Remoulade sauce.

Remolaude Sauce:

2 cups of mayonnaise
2 tablespoons Creole mustard (or any piquant mustard)
1 small grated onion
3 goodly tablespoons prepared horseradish
2 tablespoons of catchup
a little salt
Juice of one lemon
A dollop of Worcestershire sauce
Several grinds of fresh black pepper
a bit of cayenne (quarter teaspoon)
a coupla shakes of Tabasco sauce

Mix ingredients well. Chill. Serve over deep fried green tomatoes. It's also good with cold shrimp, cold ham, or roast beef. Leftover sauce can be jarred and stored in the refrigerator.

Quantity Cooking For Big Old Outdoor Parties

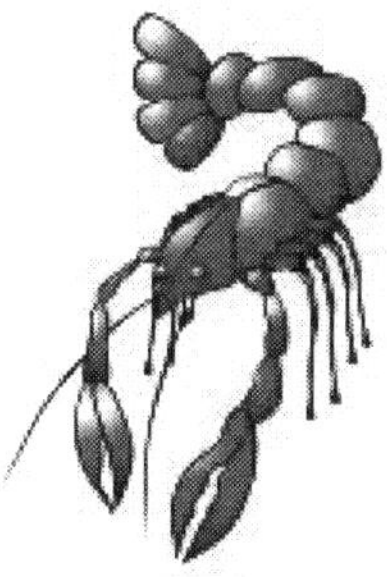

Crawfish Boil:

For cooking up about a bunch of lip smackin' *écrevisse*, the key is having a lot of cold beer on hand..

To do the crawfish or *écrevisse*:

Put a basket in a 20 gallon cook-pot half full o' water and add six ounce of cooking oil (the oil makes getting the meat outta the shell easy.) Bring to a boil on an outdoor propane burner. Add one small bottle of liquid crab boil (Zaterain's is good). Drink a cold one. Add 10-12 bay leaves and a cup of Tabasco sauce. Drink another cold one. Squeeze two dozen lemons and pour in the juice. Drop the lemon halves in too. Now add five pounds of whole red taters and several pound of onions.

Cook for fifteen minutes. Now's a good time for a cold one.

You can rinse the crawfish while you drinking the beer. Best way is put the whole 40 pound bag of crawfish in a cooler with the drain open and hose those buggers down. When the mud is gone dump them crawdads in another cooler an' rinse again. Now put them aside.

You're going to need another beer while you husk a dozen ears of' corn an' cook them for 10-15 minutes in the same pot as the potatoes and onions. .

Pull the basket with the corn and onions and potatoes, and lemon rind and put put them in a big container for' later.

Now you gonna cook the crawfish. Put the basket back in the pot.

Add:

- One sack of crawfish boil.
- The whole container of Tone's Cayenne Pepper (yep, the entire container)
- Stir the stuff for about a minute.
- Add the crawfish.
- Bring up to a rolling Boil.

Cook for about five minute, turn the heat off, and soak for 10-15 minutes. Dump on to a picnic table covered with butcher paper covering and eat 'em wit potatoes, onion, and corn. Gotta have another cold one with the écrevisse

A forty pound' bag makes 'bout 10 pounds of crawfish meat or enough for a couple of Cajun boys. Of course you can cook a smaller 'mount if you adjust the recipe. Or a bigger amount if you have a lot of folks partaking.

Yum! Eating those succulent morsels is les bon temps.

B-B-Q PIG:

Fixing a pig is easy, provided you got some guys an' a supply of cold ones.

First get a hundred-hundred twenty pound pig from a butcher-shop, a lean one that won't start a grease fire. Butterfly that t pig the day before cooking and rub it with the dry spice. Then the next day lay the pig out flat on the pit grate for the cooking.

Make the fire in advance. Use about three-four big bags of charcoal briquettes an make the fire next' to the pit so you can move the coals to the pit as you need them. Add coals to the pit all day long. Make sure the coals are all along the pit with extra ones on the ends.

Cook the hog for ten-twelve hours. You want to cook skin up for' 6-8 hours. Then two hours or so on the flip side. Finish cooking wit the skin up. Watch the temperature with a good meat thermometer stuck in one of the hams. When it gets to 170 degrees on the F scale the hog is cooked

You're gonna need a mop to baste the hog every hour or so. And sauce is added when the pig just about finished.

When the hog is done pull it from the fire and wrap it in foil. Let it set an hour or so then start pulling the meat. Cleaver up the hog into large chunks, about 5 to 10 pounds a piece. Then pull the meat, mixing it from all parts of the the pig.

The secret to a good pig is for boys to watch the fire all day (or night) to make sure the carcass don't burn. cold beers make that task easier.

That's all there is to it.

* See below for the dry spice rub, the mop, and the sauce recipes.

The Dry Spice or Pig Rub:

Mix together a half cup of ground black pepper, half cup of chili powder, half cup of sugar, quarter cup salt, four teaspoons mustard powder, two teaspoons cayenne.

Rub that spice mix all over the butterflied hog, inside and out.

The Mop:

Three quarts of cider vinegar and half that much water. Three fourths of a cup of salt and a quarter cup of chili powder. Mix them all together an mop the hog with the mixture every hour-hour an' a half.

The Cajun B-B-Q Sauce:

Make as much as you like. Experiment wit how much ingredients. Use meat stock (beef, poultry, pork) or canned broth, bacon , chopped onion , chili sauce, honey or molasses, orange juice, lemon juice, butter, fresh garlic (minced), Tabasco sauce, onion powder, garlic powder, salt, white pepper, black pepper, cayenne pepper.

Mix up the black and white and cayenne pepper, onion and garlic powder, and salt.. Fry the bacon crisp then crumble it and set aside. Add chopped onions to the bacon drippings an fry till brown. Add spice, stock, chili sauce, orange juice, bacon, garlic, Tabasco sauce and lemon juice. Cut the heat an' stir. Cook over low flame for about twenty five minutes. Put in the butter an' stir until melted. Cool off an' blend' in the processor until smooth

B-B-Q pig ain't worth the trouble without a tub of cold ones.

Pulled Pork Bar-be-Que:

Start with whole Boston Butt (pork shoulder) about nine to ten pounds. One butt should feed ten-twelve people. Cook as many butts as the crowd will need.

Remove most of the skin from the butt but leave the fat.

Make a pork rub:

Mix together a half cup of ground black pepper, half cup of chili powder, half cup of sugar, quarter cup salt, four teaspoons mustard powder, two teaspoons cayenne. Slather the butt with yellow mustard (sticking agent) and rub the spice mix all over Boston Butt the day before cooking and refrigerate.

Fire up your charcoal smoker or grill, coals offset to the sides. Two hundred to Two twenty five degrees is perfect. Put soaked wood chips in the smoker chip box (apple, hickory, whatever you like). Smoke the butts for10 to 12 hours. If done right all of the fat and gristle will be cooked away leaving only tender juicy pork.

Remove the butt(s) from the smoker, wrap in tinfoil, and let rest for an hour or so. Cleaver the butt to chunks and pull it apart with two forks. The meat will be juicy and succulent. Dress with your favorite bar-be-que sauce and warm in a low temp oven or crock pot.

Serve with Cole slaw, potato salad, buttered corn on the cob.

Lots of cold beer. A real treat. Enjoy.

Back Yard Oyster Roast:

Rightly oysters are steamed but, what the hey, we call the party an oyster roast. Oysters are in season during the "R" months, September through April. Best in winter.

You'll need a bushel of oysters (about 50 pounds) for 5 people. A large piece of sheet metal (about 3 feet square and an eighth to a quarter inch thick), four masonry building blocks, burlap sacks. Participants must have oyster knives, heavy work gloves. A couple of lined trash can are required. A stand-up height oyster table or two, or three helps. There's a hole in table and the trash can goes there.

Oysters will likely be muddy. Wash them several times with a garden hose or a pressure washer. Build a charcoal fire that fits the size of your metal top. A masonry block at each corner. Sheet metal on top of the blocks. Sprinkle a few drops of water on the metal—water sizzle indicates the top is hot. Oysters go on in a single layer.

Now, cover oysters with a soaking-wet burlap sack or two. Cook oysters 8 to 10 minutes. (shells will open about ¼ to ½ inch.) Move the cooked oysters with a new or scrubbed shovel to the oyster table. Allow the metal to reheat, repeat the process with more oysters. Add charcoal as needed.

Hungry folks can pry open oysters using an oyster knife. Loosen oyster meat. Toss the shells in the trash can. Other waste (paper towels, hot dog plates, etc.) go in a separate trash can.

Hot sauce made of catchup, horseradish, lemon juice, and Tabasco sauce is a must. Premium saltines go on the table. Also, on the table are rolls of paper towels.

An oyster roast is completed with a concoction of smoked sausage, boiled shrimp, boiled potatoes, onion boiled with butter and Old Bay or a similar seasoning. Chili, hot dogs on buns, and corn on the cob also go well. Cold beer is a must. Wine for some of the ladies. What a feast.

Burrrrrp!

Hot Dogs and Hamburgs:

Simple and delicious when cooked on the outdoor grill. Make sure you have catsup. mustard, onion. green relish, and maybe chili. Potato chips, salads (potato, cole slaw, macaroni) and cold beer and soda are needed. You can't do much better than this.

The Day After The Outdoor Party (advise to the wise).

Your place is gonna be a mess what with the folding chairs and tables, the beer bottles, the paper plates, the plastic utensils and all manner of other trash. There might even be pig or turkey carci or piles of crab or oyster or mudbug shells. Maybe even some left over, hung over guests.

So, my friends here is what you must do. Come morning, dragoon some friends to help with cleanup. Give 'em trash bags, garbage cans, brooms and rakes, and, if needed, shovels. They'll get the place shaped up 'cause they want to be invited next time.

Besides, you'll provide a couple of cold ones while they clean up. They know it, 'cause, it is the truth.

That's all folks.
Use the recipes as guides.

Experiment.

Adapt.

Concoct your own smackrels.

Most of all enjoy.

Because that's why we are here on this good green earth

Laissez les bon temps rouler.

GC Smith is a southerner. He writes novels, short stories, flash fiction, poetry. Sometimes he plays with dialect, either Cajun or Gullah-Geechee ways of speaking. Smith's work can be found in: Gator Springs Gazette, F F Magazine, Iguanaland, Dead Mule School of Southern Literature, Naked Humorists, The Glut, Flask Fiction Magazine, N.O.L.A. Spleen, NFG Magazine, Cellar Door, The Beat, Dispatches Magazine, Beaufort Gazette, Coyote's Den, Southern Hum, Lamoille Lamentations , Quiction, The Landing, The Haunted Poet, Flavor a Deux, The Binnacle, Stymie Magazine, Bannock Street Books. He has three published novels, WHITE LIGHTNING -Murder In the world of stock car racing, THE CARBON STEEL CARESS: A Johnny Donal P.I. Novel, and IN GOOD FAITH: A

Johnny Donal P.I. Novel. GC also has published a poetry chapbook: A Southern Boy's Meanderings.

Thank you for reading my book. If you enjoyed the read or cooked some of the food please write a review to leave at your favorite retailer. I'd sure appreciate your review and, I'm sure da Mudbug will as well. Thanks.

Salut!

63059452R00100

Made in the USA
Columbia, SC
08 July 2019